Run To Murder

Behavioral Unit Maine Series Book One

Bella Lane

Run To Murder Blurb

Maine has a Behavioral Unit, but will they be able to catch the Serial Killer?

Special Agent Eric Chandler, a seasoned member of the FBI's Behavioral Unit relocated his team to the city of Largo, Maine to help catch the serial killers that are operating around the State.

Dr. Michelle 'Shelly' Farrell is the State of Maine Medical Examiner. She's the voice for the victims who no longer have one.

When bodies of women start turning up dead, Dr. Farrell knows there's a serial killer running loose in the State of Maine. She turns to the ones she trusts most for help getting justice.

As the clock ticks, Eric and the team have a challenge ahead of them, finding the serial killer before he takes another victim.

Behind the façade of professionalism displayed in front of the team, Michelle and Eric have a romantic relationship. Will these two continue to keep their feelings secret or will they finally come clean to the team?

When the Serial Killer strikes again, this time it's with one of their own. Will Eric and the team be in time to save their own and catch the killer?

PLEASE READ CAREFULLY.

There are elements and themes within this book that some readers might find extremely upsetting. Please go to my website **www.be llalanebooks.com** under content warning for the list of potentially harmful topics. Please heed these as this book contains some heavy situations that some readers could find damaging.

Table of Contents

1. Prologue — 1

2. Chapter One — 5

3. Chapter Two — 13

4. Chapter Three — 25

5. Chapter Four — 35

6. Chapter Five — 45

7. Chapter Six — 53

8. Chapter Seven — 61

9. Chapter Eight — 67

10. Chapter Nine — 73

11. Chapter Ten — 81

12. Chapter Eleven — 89

13. Chapter Twelve — 101

14. Chapter Thirteen — 109

15. Chapter Fourteen   111

16. Chapter Fifteen   117

17. Chapter Sixteen   125

18. Chapter Seventeen   133

19. Chapter Eighteen   139

20. Chapter Nineteen   147

21. Chapter Twenty   153

22. Chapter Twenty-One   155

23. Chapter Twenty-Two   161

24. Chapter Twenty-Three   169

25. Chapter Twenty-Four   175

26. Chapter Twenty-Five   181

27. Chapter Twenty-Six   193

Acknowledgements   199

About the author   201

Also by   203

Prologue

UNKNOWN

Four weeks prior

I walk out onto the jogging path, trying to calm the demon inside of me. He wants to be let loose, but I need to find the faith inside me to keep him from unleashing. I sought out a therapist, in hopes that they could help me fight the demon inside.

I had hoped talking with a therapist would help me, but instead he prescribed me medication. I stopped taking them a week ago, they made me feel weird and distorted. Though the medication did stop the demon from exercising his destruction for a little while, I continued to feel his urges even more inside of me. I was left with no choice but to stop the medication. I didn't want to feel his urges.

I went to confession and like a good catholic, confessed all my sins. I had hoped the priest would help me to rid the demon inside. He told me I had to fight the demon inside, look to God, and my unwavering faith will save me. He prayed with and for me, but I can still feel the demon inside of me even stronger than before, if that's possible. He's laughing, knowing I will never be able to be rid of him.

I'm walking on this jogging path, internally praying as the priest told me to do. I'm begging God to take this demon out of me when I hear the slapping of soles as they hit the pavement behind me, and I turn my head slightly to see who it is.

I'm caught off guard, watching as she jogs toward me. The demon inside stops me in my tracks as she runs past me in her tight yoga pants that showcases her round ass. The sheen from the glistening sweat that covers her body, making her glow. The sports bra that holds her breasts in tightly, only allowing them to jiggle a little bit. I can see the hard pebbles of her nipples begging to be bitten. She turns and gives me a blinding smile, and that's all my demon needed to see.

I look around to see if anyone is with her, but there is no one else in this park or on this path. I feel my penis tighten painfully as my eyes turn and take in her long legs and tight ass. I can feel the demon inside me, he wants to feel the warmth between those legs and hear her cries.

I get pushed to the side as he takes over. He walks us into the brush, off the path and watches her continue her jog. My eyes look over at the lake that is three hundred yards down the hill. The sun is setting, making the water look like glass, and a smile forms on my face.

I count as she continues to make the loop around the path, since I first saw her, she has gone around four more times, one more pass, and she will be his. The magic number is always six.

She doesn't know I'm standing here, can't see me as I watch her from the bushes. I hear the slapping of her shoe soles as they continue to hit the pavement. She's getting close, I can feel the demon's excitement of what's to come coursing through me.

My heart is racing, my penis is hard and full. Just as she gets to the bushes where I am standing, the demon quickly jumps out and punches her in the head. She falls to the ground, a little disoriented, then he punches her in the temple, and I watch as she blacks out.

He looks around, making sure there is still no one around. I can feel him gently pick her up, carrying her like his bride. I'm trying so hard to take my body back, but the minute he feels her body against ours, he completely pushes me out of the way and takes over, carrying her through the brush and down to the trees by the lake.

There is nothing more I can do except beg God for forgiveness as the demon begins to strip her of her clothes and sink my penis inside her warm vagina. I can't lie, it does make me feel good, but also disgusted as he takes what he wants from her while she is knocked out.

I feel my lips wrap around her nipple, and my tongue flick her hardened bud, as he sucks and bites, while my hand squeezes her other breast, and the demon slides my penis in and out of her so hard.

He spreads her legs wider to get deeper inside her and continues pumping in and out of her. The words coming out of my mouth are so dirty as he talks to her, calling her his little slut and telling her how he is enjoying fucking her cunt, then I watch as she starts to stir.

Her eyes pop open as he slams into her. I watch as she begins to open her mouth to scream and fight, all while he laughs and keeps pumping in and out of her.

He grabs her wrists, lifts her arms above her head, and says, "I love the fight. Your body tightens up so much more, and it feels so fucking good."

"Stop, please stop," she calls out.

"Oh no, my little slut, I have so many plans for our time together, and though you may not enjoy it, I'm going to enjoy it all," he says as he continues to grunt, pushing into her hard.

I internally cover my ears, not wanting to hear anymore. I know what he is going to do, and even though it all makes me feel good with how tight and warm they all are, I know this is wrong, and I can't witness it anymore.

"God, please forgive me," I call out as the demon continues to laugh and grunt, while taunting the young woman with his plans for her.

Chapter One

ERIC

Present Day

I stand in front of the mirror as I wrap my tie around my neck. I take in my dark hair, which is currently damp but combed. The crisp white shirt and black slacks are pressed just right and fit my six-foot one muscular frame perfectly. I finish tying my tie and stand there looking at a man who is all business. I hear the shower turn off, wishing I had stayed in there with her a little longer.

I watch through the mirror as the door opens and see her wearing a robe while towel drying her long blond hair. She throws the towel into the hamper and then looks up at me.

"Don't you look all business," she quips with a smirk framing her lips.

My eyes drag down her body, seeing her long-toned legs peek through the bottom of the robe as she makes her way into her closet to grab her clothes for the day. I watch as she slides the robe off her five foot six slim and toned naked body, showing me her backside. I catch sight of the dimple in her lower back that I have kissed a hundred times and take in her plump round ass that is sporting my handprints right now.

The image of her on her knees as she sucked my cock deep into her silky mouth, not even thirty minutes ago, slams into my mind. Her green eyes filled with lust and desire as she looked up at me while I pushed my cock deeper into her warm mouth as the water from the shower cascaded over both of us.

I bat the image and memory away as quickly as it came. I can feel my dick getting hard in my pants, and if it wasn't for the fact that I need to get to the office before the other agents. I would bend her over in that closet and fuck her so hard again.

Nothing feels better than being buried deep inside her, feeling the warmth of her tight pussy walls as they strangle my cock, and unloading my seed inside her as I watch her come apart in my arms.

"I'll see you later?" I call out to her as I make sure my tie is straight, while grabbing my suit jacket.

"Mmmm, anything is possible, you know that, Agent Chandler," Michelle says, as she comes out of the closet carrying her outfit for the day with a smile on her lips and lust in her gorgeous green eyes, as they glide up and down my body, taking in my attire and the tent in my pants that seems to be getting harder the longer she looks at it. She licks her lips, no doubt remembering what she had in her mouth.

I watch as she lays the clothes on her bed and walks toward me, still naked. Her voluptuous breasts jiggle as she saunters over to me. I try to tamper down my desire as she lifts her head up and kisses my lips. I grab her by the back of her head, tilting it so I can take the kiss deeper. She pushes her naked body up against mine, and I reach down, lifting one of her legs as my hand glides to her ass cheek, and I squeeze. I hear her moan, feel her hand reaching down the front of my pants, and as she's about to unzip my pants so I can slide my cock inside her, her phone rings.

I set her leg down, and slowly pull back from the kiss. She sighs with a pout, then says, "Seems work is calling early." I nod as she walks over to the nightstand and picks up her phone, mouthing "later" to me as I force myself to walk out of the bedroom and leave her apartment. I head to my car, trying my hardest to calm my hard, aching dick down.

I start my car, knowing I need to get my head into work mode. There are currently twenty-seven active case files sitting on my desk from the departments around the State of Maine, requesting our help.

The Behavioral Unit is a small section within the FBI, and though there are times where we have to cross state lines, it hasn't been often since the unit moved here. Most of our cases are focused solely in the State of Maine now.

Our unit specifically deals with serial killers, and not every case that is currently on my desk involves a serial killer. I usually assess the files they send to me and guide them to the appropriate offices if I can.

Most serial killers have a brand or calling card that they leave. In order to be considered a serial killer, they must have killed at least three people, leaving a pattern to identify.

Serial killers have evolved since the days of Jack the Ripper, Son of Sam, and the Boston Strangler. They seem to use more of yesterday's techniques and today's technology against us, but for them it's the little mistakes that get them caught.

There are some serial killers that we haven't been able to narrow down and catch. Some even change their patterns to throw us off, but there is always a small clue that lets us know it is them. Even with today's technology of DNA and different testing, they seem to be smarter in what they do or how they do it. With each body that is found, the taunting seems real and weighs heavy on my mind.

There are five team members on the team, and I supervise all of them as the lead agent, though we all tend to act more as a family. In this job, you have to be able to trust the people you are working with, and they have to be able to trust that you will lead them in the right direction.

Years ago, one of ours, Matthew Thorn, left the section to work in the FBI Art Crime in D.C. He was young when he started with us, but the years in the unit took its toll. He hated that we couldn't catch a serial killer, it ate away at him. I didn't blame him for leaving, we all had a hard time with the Chillicothe, Ohio killer case, but Matt was so invested, it tore him up every time we found another body.

A few years ago, he ended up being accused of art theft, but then was found innocent. He was set up by one of our own. Some in the FBI field still think he's guilty and a traitor to the badge, but others like myself and the team members who know him, know he is innocent.

Last I heard, he moved to Largo and became a bodyguard for Top Grunt, an elite group of ex-special operation forces guys. He's married with twins and doing well for himself.

This team relocated from D.C. to Largo two years ago, as Maine needed a Behavioral Unit on ground, especially after they had a serial killer who was carving women up. The only living victim was Matt's wife, Alisa.

I haven't seen Matt in years, and since moving here from D.C., I haven't had the time to look him up. It would be nice to catch up with him, he always did have a sharp mind.

I walk into the building and get in the elevator. I use the key fob that will take me up to the fourth floor, that is dedicated to the FBI, making my way into our small area. I unlock the door that leads me into our space and take in the cubicle areas that we have dubbed as the bullpen. There is enough space for all my agents to have their own workstation, which is typical gray government furniture, and yet still be able to communicate with each other if needed. Along the left side of the room is a conference room where we hold our meetings behind a wall of glass. The rest of the building floor houses other departments of the FBI, such as our IT Department, Criminal Division, and Intelligence.

I walk to the back of the room where my office is located, and the lights come on immediately. There is a wall of windows behind my desk, allowing me to see that the morning sun is still rising, but soon the office will be flooded with so much light that the lights from above will not be needed. I have a couple of filing cabinets along the wall to the right, and a couple of bookcases on the left wall that have a few criminal law books as well as state jurisdiction laws and such. On my desk sits my computer and the case files that wait for me.

I walk around the mahogany desk and grab the first file off the never-ending pile on my desk. I sit in my chair and begin to read through it. Immediately, I know it's not a serial killer, but it is definitely a homicide. I put the file in a separate pile for the homicide division and pick up the next one.

Two hours and six files later, there is a knock on my door.

"Good morning, Eric."

I look up from the file and see Agent Kimberly Santiago standing in my door. Kim stands at five foot six, slender, with long dark hair, currently pulled back in a tight ponytail. She has dark brown eyes that rival her hair color, matching the ethnicity of her Hispanic background. She's wearing black suit pants with a cream top and a black blazer.

"What's going on, Kim?" I ask, placing the file on my desk and giving her my full attention.

"Dr. Farrell wants to see us in the morgue," she tells me.

"Do you know what it's about?" I ask.

"No, she didn't say. All she said was she needed to speak to the both of us," Kim says, looking grim.

I stand up and follow her out of my office. I see the other four agents in the bullpen at their desks, and they all look up as Kim and I make our way to the door.

"What's going on, Eric?" Agent Frankie Mathis asks.

"Not sure yet, but I'll let you all know as soon as we return," I say, still following Kim to the elevators.

Kim drives us over to the state morgue to meet with Dr. Farrell, while I sit here wondering why she wants to see us. It's not very often that she ever asks for us to come to her office building.

Kim parks the car, and we both get out, making our way into the state building, taking the elevator down to the morgue. When we walk in through the double doors, Dr. Farrell is standing beside the mortician's table, jotting down notes on a clipboard.

Her back is to us as we walk in, and I notice she's in her white doctor's coat that goes the length of her body to her knees. I see she's wearing black slacks and flats. When I left her this morning, she was still naked, so I never noticed the outfit she chose for the day.

She looks up at the two of us and says, "Thank you both for coming. I know this isn't usual protocol, but I need to bring something to your attention."

"What's going on, Shelly?" Kim asks.

Kim and Michelle have been best friends since they met in college as roommates. Kim can read Michelle, just as well as I can, and I can see how upset Michelle is, but I give her the time she needs to compose herself in order to be able to talk.

I remember the night I met Shelly. We had been in Largo for about six months, when Kim told us of a bar that her old college roommate recommended and how we should all go have a drink and unwind from the week. It was something we used to do in DC as a team, so we decided to follow Kim and check it out.

Immediately walking into the bar, my eyes are drawn to the blond sitting at the bar facing toward the door. I watch as her eyes light up, and a gorgeous smile forms on her face. She stands up as Kim walks up to her. I realize this must be her old college roommate and watch as they hug each other.

"Team, this is my best friend and old college roommate, Shelly."

"Watch it with the old," Shelly says with a laugh.

"Shelly, this is Agent Mya Morgan, Agent Declan Carr, Agent Frankie Mathis, Agent Heath Robertson, and Special Agent Eric Chandler," Kim says, pointing all of us out as she introduces us to her friend.

Shelly shakes everyone's hands as they are introduced. When she gets to me, the minute her hand is in mine, I feel the electric current shoot up my arm and straight to my groin. Her eyes light up, but ever the professional, she says, "It's so nice to meet you all. Welcome to Largo, Kim has told me so much about you all."

We decide to get a booth, and I watch as Shelly walks with Kim. I notice she's dressed in a black skirt that comes just below her knees, showcasing her phenomenal figure. The light blue blouse accentuates her large breasts, leaving my mouth watering to taste and my fingers itching to touch.

I've never had a reaction to someone like this before, and it takes everything in me to calm my raging hard on.

"So Shelly, what do you do?" Eric asks.

"I'm the state coroner for Maine, actually. Dr. Michelle Farrell."

"So, we might get to work with you on some of our cases then," Eric says.

"Anything is possible," she says with that smile that lights up the room.

It was another six months before she and I started to see each other in secret, though after a year together, we are pretty sure the team knows. Still, we maintain a professional persona in front of everyone, but it's anything but professional when we are alone.

Chapter Two

MICHELLE

I hear the door open, and even knowing who I would see standing there, it still didn't stop my knees from getting weak. God, this man is lethal in his business suit, and even though I just saw him a few hours ago, it's almost like I'm seeing him for the first time in that bar all over again.

Special Agent Eric Chandler is two years older than me at forty-four and stands at six-one, muscular, with dark hair and bright blue eyes that I swear can see all the way into your soul.

The first time I met him was when Kim brought her team to the bar. The moment he entered, it was like the air in the room was sucked out, and no one else existed but him. When he placed his hand in mine, it took everything in me not to immediately fall to my knees. The electric current shot through my body, making my pussy immediately throb with need.

Six months, we danced around each other until one night he showed up here at the office while I was doing paperwork under the guise of business, however that immediately changed the minute his lips slammed on mine.

"You really shouldn't look at me like that," he says growly, walking toward the door.

"Like what?" I respond huskily, as I take my white jacket off to hang it up, while also trying to calm my needy body.

I hear him groan, then he shuts the office door. I hear the lock click before he walks back to me, and grabs the back of my head, turning me to face him, and slams his lips on mine. I gasp in shock, giving him the opening he needs to take the kiss deeper. Our tongues battle each other, and good lord, this man tastes divine.

His hand reaches around to knead my breast through my shirt, and I feel his fingers pinch my nipple. The hardness of his length can be felt through his pants as he pushes into me. I slide my hand down to rub his bulge, shocked at how long and thick it feels through his pants.

He lifts my skirt to my waist, and I hear the ripping sound of my underwear. I quickly undo his buttons on his slacks and pull the zipper down. Pushing his pants down, I grab his hard cock and begin pumping it as his fingers pump in and out of my pussy, causing me to moan and buck.

He sits me on my desk, opens my legs, and lines his cock at my entrance.

"This is probably going to be quick," he warns me as he slams his cock into me all the way to the hilt.

"Fuck," I call out, while he waits for me to adjust to his size before moving.

"You are so tight," he tells me with gritted teeth.

"You are so huge and thick," I say back with a moan.

"I have to move."

"Yes, please," I beg him, and he does as I wrap my legs around him. He continues to pound into me, while squeezing my breasts.

"Being inside you feels better than I imagined," he grunts.

"You imagined us?" I ask between pants.

"Every." Thrust, "Fucking day." Thrust deep. "For the last six months," he grits out as he continues to pound into me.

I can feel my body tightening up and my impending orgasm. Then he pinches my clit, simultaneously telling me, "Come now," and I do as I call out his name.

"Yes, that's it," he says, and he keeps thrusting into me before he comes inside me, letting out a roar with my name leaving his lips.

It takes a few more minutes for us to get our breathing to calm down, then he asks, "Are you okay?"

"More than okay," I respond with my head on his shoulder.

"Next round will be in a bed where I can ravish your entire body, but for now, we should get dressed so we can leave."

"Next round?" I lift my head and ask him to ensure I heard right.

"Oh, I am not done with you, Doctor. I told you this one would be quick, and now that we have that out of the way, I'm ready to take my time."

I can't help the blush and excitement that courses through my body at his words.

"Unless this isn't what you want?" he asks, now looking a little unsure of himself.

"Oh, I want, I definitely want to do that again and more, but for the sake of my friendship with Kim, your team, and our professions, we should probably keep this to ourselves," I tell him.

"That will not be a problem, but know this, I do not share, so even though we will have this secret that doesn't mean you get to have other relations," he tells me, his blue eyes piercing deep into me.

"That's not a problem, since I'm not seeing anyone, but this goes both ways, caveman," I tell him as I scoot off my desk and pull down my skirt, while smoothing it.

I look up at him, and he grins down at me.

"Did you not hear when I said you are all I've thought about and wanted for the last six months? There is no one else I want to be with."

My knees go weak at his declaration, and I can't help the need that immediately takes over my body for this man.

"We should go back to my place," I whisper to him.

"Lead the way," he tells me with desire shining in his eyes back at me.

The man is gloriously lethal, and I have had the pleasure for the last year of enjoying every part of him. Though our relationship started out as a secret, Kim has hinted around plenty of times of potentially knowing or suspecting. I'm sure the rest of the team suspects as well, but Eric and I always try to maintain a professional working relationship when others are around, not that we care anymore whether they know of our relationship away from work, we just don't have the need to flaunt it.

"What's going on, Shelly?" I hear Kim ask, pulling me from my thoughts of Eric and back to reality.

I take a deep breath, knowing I'm about to dump some shit on them. "This morning, I was called out to a scene. Young girl, completely naked, in a lake. I just completed her autopsy. She was sexually assaulted and sodomized. She has petechial hemorrhaging, which suggests suffocation, but there is nothing to indicate how it was done. There are no bruises around her neck to suggest strangulation, her hyoid bone is still intact."

"DNA?" Eric asks.

"She was found in a lake, so there is no viable DNA to retrieve."

"Okay, so why are we here?" He asks gruffly, and I understand why.

I take a deep breath and then say, "I called you here, because she is the fourth victim I have received in four weeks. I believe you have a serial rapist/killer in the area."

"The local police haven't called us," he says, with a look of worry on his face.

"Probably because all these deaths happened in different counties. You know as well as I do the local law enforcement agencies don't talk to each other unless there is more than one case in each county. Right now, I have four deaths in four different counties, but all died in the same manner and found the same way."

"Were these victims drowned?" Kim asks.

"No, there is no water in any of the victims' lungs. It's almost as if they were placed in the body of water in order to contaminate any DNA that could have been on or in them."

"Did you find any semen inside them?" Kim asks.

"Maybe," I say, chewing my bottom lip as I look up at Eric and watch his eyes dilate. I quickly release my lip and try not to rub my thighs together as I stare back at him. No matter what or where we are, with one look, this man can make me needy. Just thoughts of him throughout the day fills me with so much want that by the time we are home together, the first thing I do is ride his thick cock.

"Maybe?" Eric asks, gruffer than I'm sure he intended, and when I glance down, I see the hardening of his bulge and damn if my body doesn't respond.

Immediately, I remember his question, and suddenly I'm not sure how to voice my suspicions. Especially remembering what I did this morning, and the need that my body is currently feeling right now, but looking back down at the woman lying on the slab it's like a bucket of cold water poured all over me. I think about what these women may have gone through, and it makes me want to retch.

"They may have swallowed semen, but it's very hard to tell. I have taken some samples to be tested, but what I can tell you, based on the bruises around their mouth, someone defiled their mouth hard," I say, getting the words out as quickly as I can.

I pull the sheet back on the latest victim, who looks very young, and show them the bruises that have shown up postmortem.

"Also, they all have been mutilated," I add, pulling the sheet down further on the victim. "He cut their nipples off their breasts."

"Could this be a trophy for him?" Eric questions, sounding very curious.

"I don't know yet, but I will figure it out," I say as I hand him my current files on all the women I have autopsied. "You may want to reach out to the departments, I'm sure there is more they can tell you," I add as I cover the young woman's body back up.

"Thank you, Michelle, for bringing this to our attention, we will look into these cases," Eric says softly.

"I'd appreciate it. These families are going to want to know what happened once they realize their loved one is gone, and if there is a serial rapist/killer out there, he needs to be caught before anyone else gets hurt," I say sadly.

I see Eric nod in agreement. My heart is heavy for what these women must have gone through. I feel Kim's arms wrap around me.

"Oh, Shelly. We will find this bastard," she says, giving me a hug.

I look over Kim's shoulder at Eric as I hug Kim back and watch as he nods in agreement. I can feel my shoulders slump, like the weight of the world was just lifted off by his agreement.

As much as I love my best friend, it's Eric's arms that I wish were wrapped around me right now.

I watch as he mouths to me "later," like he knows what I really need, but can't have. It's also the same thing I said to him this morning before he left, and I answered the phone. I slightly nod my head to him before pulling away from Kim.

"Thank you both," I tell them with a small smile.

"I'll give you a call later, and maybe we can go for a run, okay?" Kim asks.

"Sure," I reply.

I watch them both leave through the doors, catching Eric looking back, before he continues to walk out. I take a deep breath, then turn back to the woman currently on the table, to put her away. I've done what I can to try to bring justice, I just hope the team can find this person before he hurts anyone else.

I became a medical examiner in the hopes of getting the voiceless justice and their families' closure. This job is not for everyone, and some days, like today, this job can feel like a heavy burden. It just makes my determination to help these victims that much more tangible.

I grab all the swabs and vials that will need to be tested in the lab as well as my notes, and make my way out of the morgue and down to my office, stopping by the lab first.

A lot of this job is paperwork and reports for the state, the hospitals, the police, and to keep on hand. I walk in my office, with no windows, since we are in the basement of the building, and sit down behind my cherrywood desk. I wake my computer and begin typing in the information.

I continue working on all the reports that I need to complete when the phone rings.

"State of Maine morgue, this is Dr. Farrell, can I help you?"

"Shelly, it's Kim. Are you ready to go for that run?"

I look at my watch and see it is five pm. I shake my head, knowing I missed lunch again, but I also know a run will do me good. "Meet you at Sky Park in thirty?" I ask her.

"Absolutely," she replies before hanging up.

I shutdown my computer, change into my running gear, which consists of black yoga pants, light pink sports bra, and of course my running shoes. I make sure to lock up the office before leaving for the night.

When I pull into the parking lot, I notice plenty of cars in the parking lot today. It's currently Spring, and the weather is perfect for being in the park. The trees are covered with green leaves to match the grass, making the scenery beautiful and calming. It's not sufferably hot, but it's not insanely cold either, this is what us runners like to call the perfect temperature. Parents bring their children here to run off the extra energy they may have before getting them home to settle down for the night. There is always a group of frisbee players on the field, and it makes jogging around the park inviting.

I see Kim is already there stretching by her car, wearing her usual black yoga pants and black sports bra. I get out of my car and say, "What did you do, leave the office as soon as you hung up with me?"

"Of course, otherwise you would have beaten me here," she says with a smile as I begin to stretch.

"Did you leave someone behind?" I ask.

"Yep, but he'll be here soon enough," she says with a sigh.

I laugh at her, not able to help myself. I continue stretching as another car pulls up. I look over to see Heath Robertson getting out of his vehicle.

Heath is another Agent on Kim's team. He's five foot eleven, with dark hair, and he has beautiful golden-brown eyes. He's younger than Kim and I at thirty-six and has no problems letting the world know he is gay.

In the last year and a half, I've gotten to know Heath really well. He hangs out with Kim and I often, and though he can be very crass with his words and descriptions, he's also hilarious.

"What the hell, Kim, you just left a bitch?" he calls out, walking over to us sporting really tight and short neon pink shorts and no shirt, showcasing his eight pack abs and tight muscles.

"You were taking too long to primp. I told you I was leaving," she responds with a shrug of her shoulders.

"Do you know how many hot men come out to run? I need to be prepared."

"Prepared for what? Everyone is here to workout, not pick up," she tells him.

"See, this is why you are single. So damn negative, and you don't put in the effort. Look at your outfit."

"What is wrong with my outfit? I am wearing the same thing as just about everyone else, including Shelly," she says, offended.

"Yes, exactly, just like everyone else," he tuts.

"Hey, what's wrong with my running gear?" I ask.

"Nothing, sweetcakes. We know you aren't looking to pick up anyone," he says sweetly to me.

"Huh?" I mutter to myself.

"Well, you on the other hand are flashing, brightly I might add, in those neon, hot pink shorts, and where is your shirt?" Kim asks.

"That's because I want them to notice me. You should always flaunt what you have," he tells her, giving her a pose that makes his muscles pop.

"Well, if those shorts get any smaller or tighter, the whole world will be flashed," she quips back.

"I'm not afraid of my package. I hear it brings all the boys to the yard," he says, flashing his smile at her.

I can't help the laugh that escapes me. "You two are so ridiculous, come on, let's get this run over so I can eat. I missed lunch today."

"Oh, what are we eating tonight? Is it a meaty kabob?" Heath asks.

"I have no idea what you are eating, but I don't think a meaty kabob is on my menu tonight," I say as we start our jog on the trail.

"Well, someone is going to be disappointed," he mumbles out, then I hear him say, "Ow, what the hell, Kimmy?"

"Who's supposed to be disappointed?" I ask over my shoulder.

"Stop it, Kim, or I'm going to tie you to a tree over there and tell those men to have fun," he tells her.

"I would have thought you would rather be tied to the tree for that," she tells him.

"Oh, I wouldn't mind it at all. All those gorgeous bodies, hands, and mouths, but you would cringe instead of embracing the fun," he gives her a devilish smile, and she shakes her head.

He turns to me and says, "Shelly, we all know about your secret love affair."

"What secret love affair? My books?"

"Books? What? Hell no. I'm talking about the man who is rocking your body enough to leave marks like that," he says, pointing to my side.

I look down, not having realized Eric left bruises on me above my hips. *Shit.*

"Jealous?" I quirk my eyes up at him.

"Hell yes, I need some details."

"Not happening. I don't kiss and tell."

"Who gives a shit about kissing, I want the deets on his rod. Is he long and thick? I'll bet he is. Does he make you gag?"

"Heath, I'm not talking about my flings with you," I tell him.

"Why not, I share all mine," he says with a pout.

"We know," Kim and I say at the same time.

"I thought we were girlfriends. Share all our juicy secrets," Heath says quietly, looking a bit hurt.

"We are, but we don't have to share every detail," I say.

"That means she really likes this one," Kim says with a huge smile.

"Okay, enough about my affairs, but to answer your question first, Heath, yes, he is long, thick, and definitely makes me gag oh so good," I say, before putting on some speed, and racing down the path with a chuckle.

I hear the other two trying to catch up, and Heath saying, "I knew it."

Chapter Three

ERIC

I stand at the stove in Michelle's house, cooking dinner while she is out running with Kim and Heath. I think back on today's events.

Kim and I get back in the car. She starts it up and I immediately open the first file, reading Michelle's report on the first victim found four weeks ago in Chatam County.

Decedent: Jane Doe   Residence: Unknown

Age: Early to mid-20's   Sex: Female

Race: White

Probable Cause of Death: Suffocation

Manner of Death: Homicide

ME Preliminary Summary of Circumstances Surrounding Death

"Decedent is a female, blond hair, blue eyes, in her early to mid-twenties, five foot six, one hundred twenty pounds, found in a lake at Chuala Park in Chatam County at approximately 0830 on 25 March 2023.

Body looks to be in shape, muscle mass is toned. Body shows signs of bruising from being sexually assaulted vaginally. Anal shows signs of being sodomized. Eyes show petechial hemorrhaging, indicating suffocation. Nipples around the breasts have been removed.

There are no bruising or ligature marks found around the neck area, hyoid bone is still intact, however the bruising around the mouth suggests rough defiling. No DNA to be found, more than likely due to where the body was found, however stomach contents and throat swabs taken for the lab to analyze more."

Manner of Death - Suffocation; Cause of Death - homicide.

I flip to the next report.

Report of Autopsy Examination

Name Jane Doe

Age Between 20-25

Race White

Sex F

Cause of Death Suffocation

Diagnoses

Signs of sexual trauma to the vaginal, anal, and mouth area. Petechial hemorrhaging of the eyes indicates suffocation, hyoid bone is still intact. Nipples from the breasts have been cut and removed postmortem.

External Description

Length 66 inches

Weight 120 pounds

Body Condition Intact

Rigor 2+

Hair Blond

Eyes Blue

Teeth Natural, in fair repair

Received is the body of a well-developed, well-nourished adult female appearing compatible with the age range. The body is unclad. Nothing accompanies the body. There are no readily identifiable marks.

Injuries

Sexual trauma to the vaginal area, anal area, and the mouth area supported by bruising.

Nipples from the breast have been cut from the decedent's body.

I flip the page to read the toxicology report, noting nothing abnormal was found in the decedent's bloodstream. I close this file and open the next. The other three files are the same manner of deaths, just different females and different counties. I understand why Michelle brought us into the case. There is no denying we have a serial rapist/killer in the state of Maine.

"When we return to the office, please gather the team and have them meet us in the conference room in about two hours. I want to call the lead detectives and get more information about each of these cases before I present this to the team," I tell Kim as I close the final report.

"Yes, Sir." Kim says, pulling into our parking lot.

We both get out and go into the building, taking the elevator to our floor. I walk straight to my office to make the phone calls needed.

I call the lead detective in Chatam County, where our first victim was found, Homicide Detective Mark Burton. No answer, so I leave a message with a request for him to call me back. Then I call the next one on the list.

The detectives in each county never responded to the messages I left, so I canceled the meeting with the team, hoping to have more information tomorrow.

The front door opens, pulling me from my thoughts.

"Oh my God, what smells so good?" Michelle asks as she walks around the corner and into the kitchen.

I take in her tight workout outfit and the light sheen of sweat coating her body causing my cock to get hard instantly.

"That smells really good, but have I ever told you how sexy you look standing over a stove?"

"No, I don't think you ever have," I whisper to her, smirking and pulling her body into mine, as I kiss her lips.

She melts into me, opening her mouth and allowing me to sweep my tongue into her mouth, taking the kiss deeper while our tongues battle each other.

She pulls back from the kiss, then asks huskily, "How long until dinner? I think I could really use a shower."

"I think we should be okay for a little while," I say as I turn the burners off and lead her to the bedroom.

I turn the shower on in the bathroom, allowing the water to warm up, while I shed my clothes and help her out of hers.

"By the way, Heath saw the marks you left above my hips," she tells me.

"Was he jealous?" I ask.

"Of course he was, but he doesn't know who, he does however know that my fling is very long, thick, and definitely makes me gag oh so good," she tells me while she leans into me, lifting her head and standing on her toes to reach my lips with hers. I feel her silky, soft hand wrap around my cock, pumping it.

"Long and thick, huh?" I say as I lift her up, allowing her to wrap her legs around me, as I step us into the shower and take her lips with mine.

I slide my cock inside her wet pussy, inch by slow inch.

"Please, Eric," she begs.

"What do you want, Michelle? Tell me," I command her.

"You. More. Please Eric, I need you," she continues to beg me.

I push into her hard, causing her to scream out and moan at the same time.

"So good," she calls out.

I fuck her hard against the shower wall, while I squeeze her ass cheeks, unable to control myself, needing to get deeper inside her.

"You are so wet and tight, absolutely perfect," I tell her as I continue pumping into her.

"YES," she calls out. "Just like that."

I lean my head down and suck her nipple into my mouth, flicking her taunt bud with my tongue to make it harder, then I move to the other one.

I can feel her inner walls tighten around my cock, and I know her orgasm is not far off as she continues to bounce on my cock, chasing her release.

I slam my lips on hers, taking her moans and screams as her juices coat my cock with her orgasm, allowing me to get deeper inside her, while her tight pussy strangles my cock, then pulling my cum from my balls, and I come deep inside her.

"Fuck," she whispers catching her breath.

"Yeah," I whisper in her neck, also catching my breath.

I slowly ease out of her and set her feet on the ground, before placing her under the shower and washing her up.

She grabs the soap from me and proceeds to wash me as I wash her. Her soft hands are all over my body, then she wraps those fingers around my cock. For a forty-four-year-old man, this woman makes me feel like I'm back in my twenties. I can't get enough of her, and before I realize it, I have her turned around, hands on the shower wall as I slam into her from behind, while gripping her hips.

I fuck her until the water gets cold, and she's come multiple times before I unload my cum into her again.

"Damn woman, you are going to be the death of me," I tell her as we both quickly clean up again and get out.

"But what a death it will be," she says, smiling coyly at me.

I wrap a towel around her, and look her in the eyes, "A death I would happily take as long as you are by my side when I go."

"I wouldn't want to be anywhere else, husband," she whispers to me before we kiss.

I smile because I love hearing her call me that, and I deepen the kiss remembering the night I proposed.

"Shell, how about we get away for the weekend?"

"I could use a weekend away. Where will we go?"

"I found a secluded cabin in Cedar on the lake where we can spend the weekend," I tell her.

"It sounds peaceful and wonderful," she tells me with a smile.

"Consider it done. We will leave right after work," I tell her, before pulling her in for a kiss.

"I can't wait," she says with a sigh leaving her lips.

That evening we arrived at the cabin in Cedar, taking in the view of the lake from the back deck. I leave her there to pour us both a glass of wine and bring out a charcuterie board of meats and cheeses with plans to grill steaks in an hour.

I hand her her glass of wine, and we both sip, looking out over the lake as the last of the sun goes down. The fall weather is perfect, though I can feel the chill start to settle in the air as the sun disappears.

I look over, taking in her beautiful, peaceful looking face. I feel the box in my pocket, waiting for the right time.

"This place is perfect," she says.

"You are perfect," I say, and without thinking, I set my glass on the table and pull the box from my pocket.

I get down on one knee in front of her and hear her gasp. "Michelle, I fell in love with you the moment I walked into that bar and have fallen in love with you more and more every day. You are my soulmate, my other half, and I want to spend the rest of my life with you every day, growing old, and sharing every little moment with you by my side."

I watch as the tears fall from her eyes, then opening the box to showcase the ring, I ask the important question, "Michelle, will you do me the honor of becoming my wife and spending the rest of your life beside me?"

"YES," she calls out. "YES, I love you and want to spend the rest of my life with you."

I place the ring on her finger and kiss her deeply.

We never did have the steaks that night and spent the majority of the weekend making love.

We went to Vegas two months ago, deciding we no longer wanted to wait. We found a beautiful chapel and found a priest to marry us. Being that we are both from a Catholic background, and neither of us had been married previously, it only felt right to find a priest in the area. We agreed no Elvis impersonators would start our marriage. Her sister and my brother came as witnesses and as our family, but we have not told anyone else about our marriage.

Everyday has been a happy honeymoon for us when we step through those doors, but one day, I do want to take Michelle on a perfect honeymoon. So, eventually we will have to tell everyone what we did, and Michelle is worried about the disappointment Kim may feel when she finds out.

Those two are close as sisters, have been for so many years, and I feel bad that Shelly hasn't been able to tell her best friend about us.

I walk back to the stove and turn the burners on again, heating the food that I was preparing, and she walks into the kitchen wearing a t-shirt, leggings, bare feet, and her diamond wedding ring.

"Shell, you know we can tell everyone when you want," I say to her.

"I know, but I like having this secret for just us. They all know so much about each of us, that selfishly I only want this as something only we know and can enjoy for the other. Does that make me selfish?" she asks.

"No, hun, it doesn't. I want to shout it from the rooftops, but you are right, the minute the team finds out, we will become the mom and dad of the group."

She laughs, but says, "Exactly. I love them all, and when we agreed to keep this relationship secret, I never anticipated we would get married, but I am enjoying the secrecy as well as the questions of are they or aren't they having a relationship," she laughs lightly.

I have to chuckle, too. "It is comical, but I want you to know, I'm ready to tell everyone when you are, but I won't lie, I love having you all to myself at night. Where it's just the two of us and no, work," I tell her.

"Good, I like it too," she says with a smile.

"Go sit down at the table, and I'll bring you your plate. I know you didn't eat lunch today, did you?" I tell her playfully.

She sighs. "No, I completely got lost in work until Kim called to go run."

I nod, "Go sit down, I'll make sure you get full, before it's time for dessert."

She laughs. "You are insatiable."

"So are you, my love," I tell her as I set her plate down in front of her.

"Hmm, this smells so good," she says, picking up her fork and taking a bite.

I smile, unable to look away as she continues to eat the food that I prepared for her.

"What's wrong?" she asks.

"Nothing. I love watching you eat, the joy on your face as you taste the food is contagious," I tell her and watch her blush.

"You definitely know a way to this woman's heart," she whispers, giving me her blinding smile that I can't help the hard bulge that I am now sporting.

"Eat up, woman. I am ready for dessert," I tell her as I adjust myself.

She gets a devious look in her eyes and says, "Yes, Sir," before chuckling and taking another bite while moaning.

I take a bite of my food, and must admit, I did a better job on the sauce than I have in the past.

Conversation turns to work when Michelle asks, "Were you able to find out anything on the Jane Does?"

We had agreed early on in our relationship to keep work out of our home, but I can tell this is weighing heavy on her mind, so I respond, "No. I called all the Detectives listed in the reports, leaving them all messages to call me back. I'll try again tomorrow."

She nods her head, "I'll look in the database tomorrow and see if anything has been updated. It will be a few days before we get the toxicology report back on the latest victim, but I'm not expecting anything different," she tells me while taking another bite of her food.

I nod before changing the subject, "How about we go to the cabin this weekend?"

"The one where you proposed to me?"

I nod, giving her a smile.

"A weekend overlooking the lake sounds wonderful," she says.

"Great, then that's what we will do," I tell her with a smile, hoping she likes the surprise I have for her.

After dinner, we clean up the kitchen together, then head to the bedroom, where I show my beautiful wife how much I love her.

Chapter Four

ERIC

The next morning, I get to the office, and dial the lead detective in Chatam County, Detective Mark Burton again. This time, there is an answer.

"Homicide Division, Burton speaking," he answers.

"This is Special Agent Eric Chandler with the Behavioral Unit. I called and left a message for you yesterday. Do you have a moment to talk about a case in your county?" I ask.

"Sorry, Special Agent, I got your message yesterday, and planned to call you back today, which case are you inquiring about?"

"Female, Blond, found in a lake at Chuala Park," I respond.

"You mean Deborah Whinster's case?" he asks.

"You have a name for her?" I ask, jotting it down in my notes.

"Yes, her family reported her missing when she didn't show up to their family dinner, and the DNA results came back yesterday matching the mother's," he tells me. "What is it you want to know?" he asks.

"I have three other cases exactly like hers in other counties, leading us to believe there is possibly a serial rapist/killer in the state of Maine."

"Oh wow, I didn't know," he says softly.

"None of the counties know, and your victim was the first in the State, so I wouldn't have expected you to call around looking. Do you have any potential suspects you were looking at for this crime?"

"No. I mean we looked at her boyfriend briefly, but his alibi checked out."

"Is there any reason she would have been at that park?" I ask.

"Her family and boyfriend said she was an avid jogger, and that she liked to jog in that park after work."

I jot that information down to ask the other counties.

"Would you mind sending me your case file, including everyone you have spoken to?" I ask.

"Sure, it's not much, but I can bring you everything I have in the next hour or so."

"That would be great, but if something comes up, let me know, and I will send one of my agents over to pick it up from you," I tell him.

"I'll be there," he tells me, a little more enthusiastically than necessary.

"Call this desk number when you get here, 523-2828, and someone will come down to the lobby to bring you up."

"Okay, thank you, and I look forward to meeting you, Special Agent Chandler," Detective Burton responds.

"Same here, Detective," I tell him before hanging up to call the next county on the list.

An hour later, I have completed all my calls, and two of the neighboring counties have agreed to bring their case files over themselves, and two have agreed to allow one of my agents to pick them up.

I walk out of my office, "Frankie," I call out to my agent.

Frankie Mathis has been with the team for the last ten years, and he is one of the youngest on the team. Frankie is thirty-four, standing at six foot even with brown hair and brown eyes. He, like Matt, had joined the military service. He had joined the Army right out of High School, and when his initial enlistment was coming to an end, I offered him the same deal I did Matt when I recruited him from the Marines.

Frankie was a stellar infantry soldier, and though he can come across as cocky sometimes, I recognized quickly that it's his way of coping with things that are out of his control. Sometimes he can rub people the wrong way, especially women with his comments and bad pick-up lines.

Of course, he didn't have much of a role model growing up, his father was an alcoholic who paraded women in and out of their house after his mother left, leaving him no real female guidance in his life.

The females on the team have tried to be that for him, and I can see a small change when we go out together now.

"Hey, Boss, what do you need?" Frankie asks.

"I need you to go to these two addresses, see these two detectives, and bring back the files they give you."

"Is there a serial killer in Maine, Boss?" he asks.

"Maybe, I'm not sure yet. There are definitely some similarities in the manner of deaths of victims, but until we have all the case files from the departments, I'm not ready to label this a case yet. Once you return with the files, then we will discuss it and decide if in fact we do have a serial killer in our state," I tell him, then look at the rest of the team as they listen in.

I continue on, "Two detectives will be arriving with their own case files, and once Frankie comes back with the other two files, we will have a meeting," I tell them all before going back to my office to wait.

I sit at my desk making some notes when there is a knock on my door. I look up and see Agent Mya Morgan accompanied by an older white male, wearing a suit. He has salt and pepper hair, roughly six-foot towering over Mya's five foot five.

"Boss, you have a visitor," Mya says softly.

"Thank you, Mya," I say, standing up to meet the gentleman in front of me.

"Special Agent Chandler, I am Detective Mark Burton."

"Nice to meet you Detective Burton," I say, shaking his hand and directing him to a seat in front of my desk. "Thank you for bringing the case file."

"I'm happy to do it," he says as he hands me his file.

I open and read through his reports. The top page is a missing person report filed by her mother.

"Why didn't the boyfriend report her missing?" I ask.

"He was out of town on business and didn't know she was missing until he returned," Detective Burton replies.

"So that was his alibi?"

"Yes," is the only response he gives.

I continue reading through his report, noting the lake was near the jogging trail. Making a note to go out and see the area myself.

"She was a beautiful young girl, such a shame what happened to her," he says as I get to a photo of her.

She has a bright smile, looking very young and carefree, and I nod at his remark. She was a beautiful young woman.

"Thank you so much Detective. My team and I will go over your notes, as well as the notes from the other counties and determine if there is in fact, a serial rapist/killer in the state."

"If you don't mind, I would also like to be involved."

I look up from my files and study the man in front of me, as he continues looking at the girl's picture, then he looks up at me.

"I promised this girl's mother I would find whoever did this to her daughter, and I would like to keep that promise," he tells me with sadness shining through his eyes and causing him to look older than his current years, I would guess.

"I would assume being a homicide detective can be very taxing on your day to day," I simply say while staring at him.

"Yes, it can be, but it's also satisfying when you get the killers off the streets and the family's closure," he says, rubbing his hands over his face. "To be honest, Special Agent, this is my last case. I will be retiring in a few months, and I want to keep my promise to this mother. Go out with a win, instead of wondering what I missed."

I nod my head in understanding. He's not the first detective I've worked with who wanted to go out of their career with a win, no matter how they get it. I can see the man is tired and ready to go enjoy life, but he will always carry the nightmares of the cases with him.

"Okay, Detective, if this is a serial killer, I will allow you to be involved in the case. Once I have the other counties files and we make a determination, I will let you know, but let me make myself very clear," I start.

"I know, this will no longer be my case, where I call the shots. I understand Agent, but if I can help, I want to do that and see this case through," he tells me.

I nod. "I'll be in touch with you, Detective Burton, I promise," I tell him.

"Thank you, Special Agent, that's all I ask," he says, allowing his shoulders to slump forward.

I walk toward the door and call, "Mya."

"Yes, Boss," she calls as she walks toward my office.

"Could you please show Detective Burton to the elevators?"

"Absolutely. Detective, please follow me," Mya says softly.

"We will talk soon, Detective," I tell him, shaking his hand and watching as he follows Mya to the elevators.

I sit back down at my desk, opening the file, and look at the picture of the vibrant young woman. My heart breaks for the family of this young woman and for the other women as well.

Thirty minutes later, Mya is knocking on my door again.

"Sir, Detective..." she begins.

"Detective Harry Smith from Lorn County, Special Agent Chandler," he says, pushing his way into my office while pushing Mya out of the way. "It's a pleasure to meet you, Sir," he continues as he thrusts his hand out.

"Detective Smith, do you always push females out of the way?" I ask, not lifting my hand to shake his.

"Huh?" He asks, looking very confused.

"You just pushed my agent out of the way and into my office without waiting to be welcomed in. I have a huge problem with the disrespect that has been shown," I say, seething.

"I apologize, I didn't realize. I was just eager to get you this file for your case. I meant no disrespect," he says, lowering his hand and stepping back.

I take a hard look at Detective Smith. He's young, maybe thirty, blond hair, approximately five-ten, but seems to work out a lot—weights—judging by his muscle build. Probably been a homicide detective for two maybe three years.

"I get you are eager to make a name for yourself, but pushing your way into someone's office and disrespecting one of my agents isn't going to help you to climb a ladder," I tell him through gritted teeth.

"I'm really sorry," he says, allowing the embarrassment to showcase on his now red face. He looks over at Mya and says, "I'm really sorry."

She nods and walks away from the door.

"Take a seat, Detective Smith," I tell him sternly, but sighing deeply to get my anger under control.

I hold out my hand for the file, and he passes it over. I see the female is still listed as Jane Doe, even after three weeks.

"Have you checked the missing person's cases?" I ask.

When I'm met with silence, I look up and see the Detective's face is blanched. He quickly schools his features, clears his throat, then says, "No, sir. I, ummm, I, didn't realize I needed to do that," he stutters over his words.

I shake my head, close the file, and look him in the eyes.

"How did you plan to solve this case, Detective?" I ask.

"Umm, I was waiting on DNA to come back, with hopes that there would be a familial match somewhere in the database," he says softly.

I stare at him, not believing what I am hearing.

"How long have you been a detective, Detective?" I ask.

"Four weeks, and this is my first case, Sir." He sits up proud.

I shake my head again and pinch the bridge of my nose, while counting to ten.

I look up at him and can see the eagerness and hunger in his eyes to do a good job.

"How big is Lorn County?" I ask him.

"We have about fifteen hundred folks, Sir. It's mainly farmland."

"I see, and you didn't know the victim?"

"No, Sir. She doesn't look like anyone I grew up with, but some of the farming folks kept their kids home to work the farm, so I'm sure there are folks I have never met," he responds.

I nod, trying to keep my composure, as it seems the young detective here has not been taught anything outside of school.

"Is there not another Detective for you to shadow?" I ask.

"No, Sir. The Detective before me retired, which opened up the slot. To be honest, Agent, we don't have many murders in our county, which was why I jumped at the opportunity. I may be young, but I am willing to learn everything I can."

"You have a lot to learn, Detective. For now, I need you to reach out to missing person, and see if someone reported your victim missing. We need a name, and though waiting for DNA to hopefully tell us something, is an option, it's a long process, and it would be simpler if we had another DNA to compare hers too. We need to find answers for this victim as soon as possible," I tell him.

"Yes, Sir. I will make the phone calls now and check the database. If I find something, I will let you know, Sir."

I stand up, "It's a good start, Detective," I say before going to the door, "Mya?"

"Yes, Sir."

"Please take the Detective to the elevators."

She nods, and I look back at the Detective, "I'll be waiting for your call," I tell him.

"Yes, Sir," he says, then looks at Mya sheepishly, "I really am sorry about earlier."

"Follow me, please," she replies.

I shake my head before grabbing both files and walking toward the conference room. I understand new detectives are eager and hungry for a win, but this one is going to need his hand held before he will ever be able to solve a case.

I pull my team into the conference room to tell them of our current findings and potential for a serial killer.

"Can we know what is going on now, Boss?" Frankie asks.

"A couple of days ago, Dr. Farrell called requesting our assistance. She had been called out to four different counties around the state, in four weeks, to find female victims, brutally raped and killed. Their bodies were left in the nearby lakes in the vicinity of parks," I say, allowing the team to pass the medical examiner's reports around.

"This says they each were suffocated, but no signs of strangulation," Frankie says, "How is that possible?"

"She doesn't know, but she is working on figuring that out," I answer him.

"And no viable suspects," Heath relays, looking through the detective files.

"It would seem that is the case, and unfortunately, we still do not know who three of the victims are," I add.

"Maine is a breeding ground for serial killers because they can get lost in the area amongst all the vegetation," Kim says nonchalantly.

"That is true, and one of the main reasons we were chosen to relocate here," I admit.

"How should we start?" Declan asks.

"We need to go and visit each of these sites, sketching the scene as it is, taking pictures and videos to make sure we don't miss anything, and then bring everything together and see if we can fit the puzzle pieces. Kim and Declan, you take Chatam County. Contact Detective Mark Burton and let him know that you will be going out to the scene. See if he will meet you there and walk you through what he found that day. Heath and Frankie will take Lorn County, contact

Detective Harry Smith. The kid is young, knows nothing about being a detective, maybe you can help each other out."

Mya snorts, "Good luck," she says softly.

"Mya, I would like for you to go through each of the reports, medical and detectives, column the similarities and the non, let's see if we can build a profile."

"On it," she says, pulling the files away from the other agents.

"Tomorrow you all will go visit the other two counties, then we will bring everything together. Any questions?"

"No, Boss," they all say in unison. I shake my head, as they disperse to their assignments.

Walking back to my office, I look at my phone, wishing I could call Michelle, but there is nothing I can tell her right now. I can only hope that the weekend away will help her get her mind off of it. I decide to go through some more of these case files, while everyone else is focusing on the tasks given to them.

Chapter Five

MICHELLE

This morning, I left the apartment a little earlier than I normally do. My mind has been heavy with the victims all night. I tried to leave work outside the door as Eric and I agreed when we first started seeing each other, but after our romantic time together last night, I couldn't help the thoughts that invaded my mind.

I'm sure Eric knew, he knows me so well, and for a few hours last night he was able to help me forget, though it didn't last. I'm looking through my emails and see one from the state lab.

DNA results from Jane Doe and Laura Whinster.

One hundred percent familial match – Laura Whinster is the biological mother.

I quickly pick up the phone and call Chatam County.

"Detective Burton," he answers.

"Detective Burton, this is Dr. Farrell from the State Morgue."

"Yes, doctor, what can I do for you?"

"Did you receive the DNA results on the Jane Doe?"

"Yes, ma'am, received them last night, and I will be contacting the family shortly to inform them that we have their daughter, Deborah."

"Okay. Could you please ask them which funeral home we should escort the deceased to and let me know?"

"Yes, ma'am. I will call you back shortly," he tells me before hanging up.

I place the phone down and rub my head. I have a name for the first victim, and my heart breaks more for her family. I know I need to prep the body for transport, but I wait for the Detective to call back and continue working through my emails.

Twenty minutes later, my phone rings, and I answer, "State of Maine Morgue, Dr. Farrell speaking."

"Dr. Farrell, it's Detective Burton, the family would like her transported to the Crowley Funeral Home in Chatam County."

"I will call the funeral home and make the necessary arrangements to get her there. Thank you so much Detective."

"Yes, ma'am," he says as he hangs up.

I call the funeral home to make sure someone will be there to receive Ms. Whinster before I fill out the appropriate documentation that will need to escort the body.

"Crowley Funeral Home. This is Dan, how may I be of service today," he answers.

"Hi, this is Dr. Farrell from the…" I don't even get to finish.

"Dr. Farrell, I can't believe I am speaking with you. I am a huge fan, and have been to every convention you have ever spoken at. What can I do for you today?" Dan asks very enthusiastically.

"Umm, thank you. I appreciate that. The family of a loved one has requested you as the funeral home to bring their loved one. I'm calling to ensure someone will be there to receive the deceased," I say.

"Absolutely, Dr. Farrell. Will you be transporting yourself?"

"No, I'm afraid not, but one of my staff will be."

"Oh, what a shame. I had hoped to be able to meet you in person, but I understand, you are a very busy and important doctor. Can I get the name of the deceased, please?"

"Thank you for the kind words and understanding. The deceased is Deborah Whinster."

"Oh no. I know her parents, oh they must be so devastated. I knew the young woman was missing, but I had really hoped she would be found. She was such a lovely young girl," he says.

"Sounds like you knew her pretty well, I'm sorry."

"Yes, our families attend the same church, St. Paul's Catholic church. This is absolutely devastating; I will need to call them immediately. Please let your driver know we will be here waiting to receive Ms. Whinster, Doctor."

"Thank you. It will take me about thirty minutes to do the transport paperwork and get her ready for transport. They should arrive within the next two hours."

"We will be ready, and thank you for calling Dr. Farrell," he says, no longer sounding eager and excited.

I hang up the phone and begin the paperwork needed to transport Ms. Whinster.

Forty-five minutes later, Ms. Whinster is on her way to Chatam County, and my heart is so heavy, knowing this is going to devastate numerous people there.

There is a knock on my door, causing me to look up from my computer. It's my assistant, Janine, standing there.

"Come in, Janine," I say as I go back to the computer screen.

"Dr. Farrell, I have the toxicology report on the latest Jane Doe that was brought in," she says, handing me the piece of paper before turning to leave my office.

"Thank you, Janine," I say, looking over the notes, and it's exactly what I expected, everything is normal. I sigh, placing the piece of paper on my desk and rubbing my eyes. I can only hope Eric is getting more answers than I am.

Hours later, my phone beeps with an incoming text from Kim.

> Drinks tonight at McKellan's?

I sigh, knowing I could definitely use a drink or two tonight. Looking at the time, I see it's four thirty. I shoot back a reply.

> I'm in, meet you there in thirty minutes?

> Perfect

she responds.

I finish up the paperwork I am currently working on, then shutdown my computer. Grabbing my purse off the coat rack, I lock my office door.

"Janine, I'm leaving for the night," I call out to her.

"Okay, have a good night, Doctor," she calls back, cleaning up her station.

I make my way to the elevator, just as Chad, the transport driver comes in from the loading dock.

"Did you have any issues with the transport of Ms. Whinster?" I ask.

"No, Doctor. The funeral home accepted her, and I have the signed paperwork right here," he tells me.

"Perfect, just place it in the inbox, and I'll file it in the morning," I tell him as the elevator door opens.

"Will do, have a good night, Dr. Farrell," he tells me walking down the hall.

I get in the elevator, pressing the first-floor button, and sigh, knowing the family will be able to put their loved one to rest. I wish I had answers for the other three women still in my morgue.

I walk out to the parking lot, blinded by the sunlight. I forget how dark things can be down in the basement. I pull my sunglasses out of my purse, putting them on, and making my way to my car.

I get to the bar, and Kim is already seated in a booth, waiting for me. I order my drink from the waitress before I sit down.

"Is it just us today?" I ask.

"No, the others will be here soon enough," she replies, and I nod.

The waitress brings me my glass of wine, and I take a sip.

"How are you doing?" Kim asks.

"I don't know, to be honest. I found out who the first victim was today, had her transported to the funeral home as requested by the family, but I still have three Jane Does lying in my morgue. So on one hand, I'm happy a family has some closure, but on the other there are still three families who don't know," I tell her while taking another sip of my wine.

"I get it," she says, and I know she does.

The door opens, and I see the rest of the team walking in.

"I take it Agent Chandler told everyone about my suspicions?" I ask.

"Yeah. It's going to take some time to piece everything together to determine if we do have a serial killer, though there is no denying the similarities of the deaths."

I nod, and the rest of the team takes their seats around Kim and I.

I glance up at Eric as Heath takes a seat next to me. I watch as he quickly masks his annoyance at not being able to sit next to me. I quickly take a sip of my wine to cover up the laughter that wants to fly out.

"We should do something fun this weekend," Heath says.

"What do you have in mind?" Kim asks.

"Maybe go up to the lake with jet skis and spend the day in the water," he says, shrugging.

"Well you are going to have to do it without me," I tell him.

"Why?"

"I'll be out of town this weekend," I respond.

"Is it with mister long and thick?" Heath asks.

"Really?" I look at him.

"What?" he asks, looking offended.

"Why do you assume I'm going out of town for a man and not work?" I ask.

"Work is boring, a man is so much more fun," he says with a twinkle of mischief in his eyes.

"You know she loves doing those speaking conferences," Kim says.

"I know, but.." he pouts, then says, "Maybe you'll meet a hunk there to save your weekend," he grins.

"My weekend will be just fine," I tell him with a laugh.

"Eric, you want to go to the lake with us," Heath asks him, but Eric only gives him a look that says seriously.

"Okay, fine, don't go, but this could be the last time we get to have some fun if these cases turn out to be what we think they are," he says, pouting, and my heart drops again.

"I'm sure you will make the most of it, Heath," Eric says.

"Damn right I will, how about the rest of you?" Heath asks.

"I'm in," Kim says.

"Why not," Mya says.

"Sure," Declan responds.

"Well I better go to keep you all out of trouble," Frankie says, and everyone laughs.

"What?" he asks.

"You do know that it is the other way around, we will have to keep you out of trouble," Kim says.

"We'll keep each other out of trouble," he says, and everyone laughs.

I finish my glass, and bid everyone good night. Eric left fifteen minutes ago, and I want to get home to him.

Chapter Six

Eric

I'm so lost in reports, that when Kim knocks on my door, I get startled.

"Hey, Boss, we are going to McKellan's for a couple of drinks, you want to go?"

I look at the time and see it's a quarter till five, and I'm sure Michelle will be there, so I scrub my hands across my face and say, "Yeah, I could use a drink before calling it a night."

"Great, see you there," she says, before retreating from my door.

I finish with the current case file in my hand, shut down my computer, grab my jacket, and walk out of my office. I meet up with the rest of the team at the door of McKellan's, and when we walk in, I find Kim and Michelle sitting down at the big booth with a drink in hand.

I watch as Heath climbs in next to Michelle, and I have to curb my reaction when the anger and annoyance hits me. I catch Michelle looking at me, and I know I have nothing to worry about, not that I really did from Heath.

Heath, Kim, and Michelle are all close, but I hate that I can't show affection to my wife, or even sit next to her while we are in a bar with the team around. I watch Michelle stifle a laugh behind her glass of wine and know I am being an idiot right now. I take a sip of my drink and continue feigning a look of indifference, though it's far from what I feel on the inside.

Heath brings up weekend plans, and my mind immediately jumps to how Michelle will feel about my surprise for her. I hope she will love it. I quickly finish my drink, knowing Michelle won't be much longer behind me. I want to get home and start dinner for the both of us, then relax with my wife. We only have two more days until the weekend, and I can't wait.

It's finally Friday, and we still have no identities of the three female Jane Does in the morgue, but my mind is on my surprise for Michelle. Since Michelle told the team at the bar the other night that she will be out of town, she thought it would be smart if she drove out to the cabin after work herself, and I would follow.

I gave her the combination code to the cabin and told her I would pick up dinner for us. I already have both our bags in the trunk of the car. I can't help the excitement flowing through me knowing I will have my wife to myself for the whole weekend. Though she alluded to the team she was speaking this weekend, she never really told them that was what she was doing, they only assumed, but at least I know they won't call her this weekend.

I park the car next to hers when I arrive, grab our bags out of the trunk and make my way into the cabin. I find a bottle of wine open on the island, and I know she is already sitting on the back deck overlooking the lake.

I put our bags in the bedroom, then go back out and get the groceries from the car. Before I get to the car, another car pulls up, and I see Jessi Valentini behind the wheel. I watch as she climbs out of the car with her bag.

"Hey Eric, how are you doing?"

"I'm good, Jessi, you caught me at a good time. I'm just getting in."

"I see, well I won't keep you long. I have the paperwork already for you to sign, then I'll file the papers, and this property is yours."

"Excellent," I say with excitement.

"Have you told your wife yet?" Jessi asks.

"No, I planned to surprise her with the news this weekend, so your timing is perfect," I tell her, and she laughs.

"If my husband did something like this behind my back, I don't know if I would kiss him or kill him," she says through her giggles.

"I've seen you with your husband, you would kiss him," I tell her knowingly.

Roman Valentini is the Chief of Police, and his wife Jessi owns the real estate business with her two best friends here in Cedar.

"You are right, plus I need him to take care of these kids he keeps wanting me to have," she says as she rubs her small baby bump.

"Congratulations, what is this, baby number three?" I ask.

"Four," she says with a sigh, but smiles brightly.

"Yeah, I wouldn't kill him yet, if I was you," I tell her with a laugh as I sign and initial everywhere she is pointing to.

Once the documents are signed, she passes me a copy of the unsigned doc, and tells me, "I'll have a copy of the signed version dropped off to you this weekend."

"Sounds good, thank you, Jessi, and tell your husband I said hi," I tell her picking up the groceries from the backseat.

"I will, and enjoy your weekend. Congratulations," she calls out before getting back into her vehicle and driving away.

I walk into the cabin and unload all the groceries, before pouring myself a glass of wine and meeting my wife on the back deck.

I see her sitting in the chair, staring out over the water, her glass on the table beside her. The last rays of the sun drifting across the water, looks serene.

"Good evening, Mrs. Chandler," I say, causing my wife to jump a little.

I chuckle before I bend down to kiss her lips.

"Hmmm," she moans, as I deepen the kiss, before pulling back and taking the seat opposite her.

"I'm sorry, I didn't hear you come in. I guess I was lost in the peacefulness of this place," she says, picking up her glass and taking another sip.

"I understand, love, and I'm glad to see you relaxing. That is the point for this weekend to relax and unwind," I remind her.

"I know, and I am so grateful you were able to get this place again. It's absolutely perfect, and to be honest, I hate when we have to leave."

"I know, and now you'll be able to enjoy it whenever you want," I casually say.

"What do you mean?" she asks, but I smirk as I can a sip of my wine.

"Eric, what did you do?"

"You know I never did give you your wedding gift," I say instead of answering her question directly.

"I don't need a wedding gift, you and your love are all I ever need," she says, leaning over the table.

"You are the best gift and partner I could have ever hoped for," I tell her, kissing her lips.

When I break the kiss, her eyes are drunk with lust and need.

"Come on, wife, I want dessert before I make us dinner," I tell her, lifting her up from the chair and grabbing our wine glasses to take back inside.

I put the glasses on the counter and notice her looking at the purchase documents that I purposely left on the island.

"Eric, what is this?" She asks. "Are you planning to buy this cabin?"

"I already did, my love. I signed the papers while you were sitting on the back deck. Jessi will have the signed copies dropped off over the weekend, but this is your place now, and you can come here whenever you want."

"Really?" she asks, with unshed tears shining in her eyes.

"Really. I know how much you love this place, and I want you to be able to come here and relax whenever you want. This will be our private getaway," I tell her.

"I love you, Eric. Thank you, it's the best wedding present ever," she says before slamming her lips on mine.

"I thought you didn't want a wedding present," I say jokingly.

"We will enjoy this one, and we should start now," she says, before pulling back and unbuttoning the buttons on her shirt very slowly. I can't help but stare at my beautiful wife as she seductively undresses in front of me in our kitchen. She slides her shirt off her, before pushing her skirt down to pool around her feet, leaving her standing in front of me in only her white lace bra and underwear.

"I love the way your mind thinks, Mrs. Chandler," I say, my voice thick and husky. I unbutton my pants, allowing my hard cock to spring out so she can see exactly what she does to me.

I watch her eyes dilate, and she licks her lips, but before she can do anything, I scope her up and lay her down on the island, pulling her bottom close to the edge. "I did say I wanted dessert before dinner," I growl before sliding her underwear down to reveal her glistening swollen pussy to me.

I push her legs down, making them open wider, as I part her folds and lick up to her clit with my tongue.

"Mmmm," I moan from the taste of her on my tongue.

I flick and suck on her clit, while I slide my fingers inside her, finding her wet and ready for me. I pull my fingers out and suck her juices off them. "Perfect," I say as I kiss her pussy before sticking my tongue inside and fucking her.

I peer up at her, as I continue eating her out. Watching as her back pushes up from the island, and she watches me while my tongue continues to fuck her pussy alternating between slow and fast. I can feel her orgasm nearing, but I want to take my time with her before she comes.

"Oh my God, Eric, please," she cries out, begging me.

I continue to tease and take my time with her, then all of the sudden she loses control, grabbing my head, pushing me into her pussy, while thrusting her hips up, and she rides my face, chasing her release.

"Oh God, Yes, like that, don't stop," she calls out as she drops her head back, still fucking my face.

I slide my thumb over her clit, applying a small amount of pressure. I can feel her legs start to shake and I know she is really close. My cock is hard, and as much as I want her to come in my mouth, I would prefer she come on my cock more. I push her hand off me, pull back my head, wipe my face. I line my cock at her entrance, and before she can say anything, I slam in her to the base of my cock.

"OH GOD," she screams, and I can't help the moan that escapes me with how tight and good she feels.

"Fuck, yes," I moan, pulling back to the tip of my cock and then slamming back in over and over again.

"YES," she cries. "Faster."

I begin to pump in and out of her like a mad man needing some release. I grab onto her hips, as she holds on to the side of the island, and I continue to pound into her until her orgasm explodes within her.

"HOLY," she calls out, as she shakes with the massive orgasm.

I'm unable to last much longer, her walls are like a vice grip on my cock, and though it feels so damn good, I can feel my balls tightening up before I come deep inside her.

"Fuck," I moan out with my orgasm.

We both take a moment to get out breathing under control, before she leans up, and I kiss her lips.

"At least we know the island is sturdy," she quips.

I chuckle, "I will not look at it the same way again, and I can't wait to lay you out on it again."

I help her off the island, and we go take a shower together. We went hiking and enjoyed the area for the rest of the weekend, and true to my word, it wasn't the only time I had her on the island.

Chapter Seven

UNKNOWN

I beat the side of my head, trying to get the demon out of me. His voice keeps taunting me, he won't leave me alone. I see the cathedral ahead and make my way to it. When I walk into the nave my eyes search out for what I am looking for, and then I see it, the confessional. I make my way over as the demon keeps taunting me.

You will never be rid of me, your Lord can't help you.

"Yes, he can and will," I seethe back to him, walking into the box. I sit and wait for the priest.

I hear the other door open and close, then the screen opens, "In the name of the Father, Son, and Holy Spirit. Amen. Welcome my Child, what can I help you with."

"Bless me Father for I have sinned. It has been seven days since my last confession. I confess I have a demon inside of me, Father, and he will not leave me. He makes me do bad things."

"What type of things, my child?"

"He makes me hurt people, he taunts me Father, and says the Lord doesn't love me."

"That is not true my child, the Lord loves us all. How does the demon hurt people, my child?"

"I'm sorry, Father," I say as I break down crying. "He makes my body do things I don't want to, Father. He says the foulest things in my head. I have prayed hard, Father, for our Lord to take the demon out of me, but the demon is strong, Father."

"You must fight the demon and sin that is inside you, let our Lord know how much you love and respect him."

"O God, be merciful to me, a sinner. Please help me to rid this demon inside of me," I pray before I leave the confession, not waiting for the priest to absolve my sins, because I know my sins cannot be absolved as long as the demon is going to continue hurting people.

I leave the cathedral as quickly as I entered and see the park nearby. This makes the demon giddy as we make our way to the park. I pray that no one is there, so he can't hurt anyone tonight.

As I walk on the jogging path, my prayers seemed to be answered, no one is here. We walk through the bushes to the lake nearby, taking in the water that looks like glass. It's so peaceful here that I begin to pray hard to my Lord that this demon can be exterminated from me.

You know you will never be rid of me. What I do is what we both really want, and you know you love the feeling we both get. It's the perfect high.

"No, I don't, you hurt them," I mutter to him.

We walk toward the bushes, when I hear the slapping sound of soles on the pavement.

"No, please, don't let it be," I pray, but my prayers are not answered.

Running by us is a young blond woman, and I can feel the demon's excitement as he continues to watch her from the bushes while she makes her laps, waiting for the sixth lap.

I relapse into the back of my mind, knowing I can no longer fight him. His breathing is picking up with the excitement of what is to come. I feel my hand rubbing my penis, making it harder, as he continues to watch her. I can hear his thoughts as he goes over the plans he has for her.

On the sixth lap, he knocks her out, picks her up, and takes her to the trees by the lake. Like the others, he quickly undresses her, before opening her legs wide, and slamming inside of her.

"Oh, so fucking tight," he says, then he pulls back, and I see blood. "Oh, she was a virgin, hmmm, so perfect for us," the demon says slamming back inside her.

"Why are you doing this?" I ask.

"You know why," he says as he grunts, pumping in and out of her, as he latches on to her nipples. "This one feels and tastes so good, I may play longer than I did with the others. I'll have her enjoying it before the end," he says, moaning and grunting.

"Wakey, wakey my pet. I want you to enjoy this as much as I am," the demon whispers into her ear while lifting her leg higher, pushing deeper inside her.

After another five minutes, she begins to moan, as he squeezes one breast, while sucking on the nipple of the other, and still pumping in and out of her.

"That's right, baby, wake up, I want you to feel what I'm doing to you," he tells the girl.

She opens her eyes at his voice and stares at him.

"I have so many plans for us tonight. I can't wait to teach you everything, and you are going to enjoy learning," he whispers to her. "Your pussy feels so good," he tells her, lifting her ass up pushing two fingers into her backend, as he pushes his cock deeper inside her.

"Oww, why?" she calls out with tears coming down her face.

"Because you are perfect, and I am the devil," he admits with a laugh.

"I'm going to make you come all over me, then I'm going to fuck this tight ass," he tells her as he pumps into her, grunting, while the only other sounds is skin slapping and her crying out.

"Nooo," she calls out as she comes hard.

"YES, that's it, my little come slut. So fucking good," he tells her before pulling out of her pussy, turning her around, lifting her ass, and pushing his cock into her tight back hole.

"No, stop, please stop. God, please, make it stop," she cries out.

He slaps her ass, then slams his cock deep into her, enjoying her screams. "God can't help you now, no one can. We are all alone with no one to hear your cries but me," he tells her, sounding gleeful as he continues to pump in and out of her.

"So damn perfect," he calls out, gripping her hips, though ensuring not hard enough to leave bruises, even though that is what he wants.

He wraps one hand around her mouth, sticking two of his fingers inside her mouth, telling her, "Suck them," while he continues to push into her ass.

He can feel his spine tingle and his balls tightening up. Damn he hasn't felt this in a long time. He learned long ago how to control his release, but he knows he's close to coming now. Her body is perfectly tight and feels fantastic. He's only had a virgin twice before, and that was so long ago, he completely forgot what it felt like, and now he's feeling like an inexperienced virgin all over again.

There is something about knowing no one else has ever felt this before. He decides he wants to play with her for as long as he can. The sun has gone down, and night has fallen, he knows no one will see him, so he allows himself to come in her ass as he grunts his release.

"Mmmm, we are going to do that again, my sweet little pet. I am nowhere ready to be done with you and your sweet body," he tells her as he pulls out of her ass.

He pulls his fingers out of her mouth and inserts them into her pussy, while he waits for his cock to harden again, knowing it won't be long, because he needs to feel her again, before he has to end it permanently.

Chapter Eight

MICHELLE

It's Monday, and I'm back in the office, relaxed and giddy from my weekend away with Eric. I still can't believe he bought the cabin, but I am so happy he did. I love that house and what it represents for us.

We christened every room over the weekend as well as the back deck overlooking the lake.

My desk phone rings, bringing me out of my memories of the weekend, and I answer, "Dr. Farrell."

"Dr. Farrell, this is Detective Caulder from Pritchard County. We have a deceased naked female found in a lake at Wyndam Park."

"I'm on my way, Detective. It will take me about an hour to get out there," I tell him while picking up my cell phone.

"Yes, ma'am. We will be waiting here for you."

I hang up the office phone and dial Eric's number from my cell phone.

"Special Agent Chandler," he answers, letting me know he is not alone.

"It's Dr. Farrell. Another female has been found in Pritchard County at Wyndam Park. Sounds like it could be another victim if you and the team would like to meet me out there."

"We will meet you there, thank you, Dr. Farrell," he responds before hanging up.

I sigh before placing my phone in my pocket. Sometimes, like today, I wish we could be honest with everyone. I need the soft Eric, especially now, kind of already knowing what I'm going to find when I go out there.

"Janine," I call out, walking out of my office.

"Yes, Dr. Farrell," she calls back.

"We need to load up, we are going to Pritchard County," I relay as I walk toward the loading dock where the medical examiner van is parked.

"Yes, Doctor," she calls out, grabbing her case, another technician, and following me out.

It takes us fifty-five minutes to get to the park, and as we pull up, I see Eric and his team getting out of their vehicles, letting me know they just arrived as well.

I get out of the van with Janine, and we walk through the shrubs to get to the body and assess it.

"Detective Caulder?" I ask the gentleman standing close by, writing in a notebook, as he takes in Eric and his team.

He looks to be in his early forties, black male, maybe five foot nine, with a round middle. Currently he's sweating profusely, letting me know he's not in the best of shape, since the temperature outside is only seventy-four degrees, not hot enough to make you sweat like that.

"Yes, ma'am, are you Doctor Farrell?"

"I am," I say, looking over the victim's body.

"Do you always bring an entourage of people in suits with you?" He asks with disdain.

I wave Eric over, and when he is close enough, I look at Detective Caulder.

"Detective Caulder, let me introduce you to Special Agent Chandler of the Behavioral Unit, Agent Chandler, this is Detective Caulder of the Pritchard County Homicide Division."

They shake hands, though Detective Caulder doesn't look happy having Eric here.

"Detective, I called the Behavioral Unit out here, because this is the fifth female victim in five weeks. I have asked his team to look into these cases for a potential serial rapist/killer."

"What? This is the first body like this in my county," he says gruffly.

"But the fifth case in the state of Maine," Eric replies calmly.

"I wanted him and his team to see the crime scene from the beginning to assess the type of person who could do this," I continue speaking as if I was never interrupted.

I get down and look into the victim's eyes, there are signs of petechial hemorrhaging, her nipples have been removed, and I'm sure we are going to find the same manner of sexual assault as we did on the other victims.

"Janine, please get the body ready for transport to the state morgue," I tell her before standing back up.

"Do you believe her death to be the same as the others?" Eric asks.

"Yes," I respond softly, then clear my throat remembering who is around. I look up at both Eric and the Detective, "She has petechial hemorrhaging of her eyes, but again, no obvious signs of strangulation. Her nipples have been removed, and I'm sure when I do the examination, I will find she has been sexually assaulted, though the fact that she has no clothes on would already lead me to that conclusion."

"But you can't be one percent sure that she is like your other victim's or that her case is related to a serial killer," Detective Caulder says.

"Just by the current examination, I can conclude her outward appearance is exactly like the other victims, but I'll know more once I do the autopsy, Detective," I tell him with a sigh, not really wanting to get caught up in jurisdiction issues.

"Detective Caulder, if this turns out to be the work of the serial rapist/killer, then us being here at the start of the investigation is exactly where we need to be, but should this turn out to be a random copycat killing, that no one knows about, then I will allow you and your department to handle the case on your own, as you do with the rest of your cases," Eric says, but with authority in his voice that makes my body break out in shivers.

God, I love when his voice is so commanding. I quickly look away from the two gentlemen, needing to get my body in check and take in the scene surrounding the body of water. There are a couple of trees close to the water, gorgeous green grass that we are currently standing on, and then a line of bushes that separate the park area from the lake area.

This looks almost identical to the last four parks I have been to, I think to myself. I look over toward the jogging path and the rest of the park, which is almost obscured by the bushes.

"Who found the body?" I hear Eric ask.

The detective sighs deeply, knowing he will not win his argument to keep the case out of the FBI's hand. "The two priests over there being interviewed by one of my detectives."

He looks down at his notebook and says, "Father Callahan and Father Mullen."

I watch as Eric walks over to the priests and the detective. Detective Caulder looks at me and asks, "Do you really believe this is part of a serial killer?"

"Unfortunately, Detective, I do," I tell him before turning to make my way back to the van that should now be loaded with our victim. I turn back around and tell him, "I'll send you a copy of my report once I've completed the autopsy, but it would be nice to have a name for the victim."

"As soon as I find out, I'll let you know, Doctor."

I nod, and continue to make my way back to the van. I'm not looking forward to doing this autopsy, because I already know what I will find.

Chapter Nine

Eric

I leave Michelle with Detective Caulder and make my way to the priests and the detective conducting the interview. I hear the detective ask the priests, "How did you happen to be in the park today?"

"Father Mullen is visiting from another parish, and the church is on the other side of the park. I thought we could talk about plans for Palm Sunday Mass while we enjoyed the beautiful weather," Father Callahan offered.

"What did you do when you found the body?" the Detective asks.

"I called 9-1-1 while Father Mullen went into the water to try to save the young woman. He pulled her to the bank, and started CPR as the dispatcher told us to do, but it was no use, the young woman was gone," Father Callahan says softly, and I watch Father Mullen look down at the ground as if he is praying, which he may very well be doing as he clutches his rosary beads.

"What did you do next?" the Detective asks.

"Once we realized the young woman was gone, we immediately recited the after-death prayer and waited for the police to show," Father Mullen finally speaks.

"Have you ever seen the victim before?" I interrupt, which causes the detective's head to snap up.

I ignore him for a moment as I continue looking at Father Callahan.

"She looked a little familiar, but I can't place where I have seen her. I try to get to know all my parishioners, but we conduct different masses, it's very hard to keep up with names, and I'm not as young as I used to be," he says.

"Has anything happened lately that stuck out to you as odd?" I ask.

"I.." he starts as his eyes light up, then says with a sigh, "No, not that I can recall," but I feel like there is something he is not saying, and I look down and notice he is rubbing his rosary beads frantically. I'm not sure if he really has memory problems or if there is something else.

"Excuse me, who are you?" the Detective asks before I can ask the priest another question.

"It's okay, Brandon," Detective Caulder tells him as he walks up to us. "This is Special Agent Chandler from the Behavioral Unit," he adds.

"Oh," Brandon says as he looks down at his notes. He's a young detective, probably new to homicide.

"Can we go back to the church now?" Father Callahan asks. "We would like to light a candle for her young soul."

Detective Caulder looks over at me, and I nod my head slightly. I know I will get nothing more from the priest at this time.

"Of course, Father. If we have any more questions, we know where to find you. How long will you be in town, Father Mullen?" he asks.

"I planned to leave after Sunday's service, but I can stay a little longer if you need me to," he offers, sounding a bit defeated. Probably due to trying to save a female he was unable to revive.

"I don't think that will be necessary, Father, as long as we have a good contact for you, should we have any more questions later on," Detective Caulder tells him, and I agree.

"Bless you my children, peace be with you, and may God be with you in finding your answers," Father Callahan tells us, before he and Father Mullen walk away.

"And with you, Father," I respond back.

"Why is the Behavioral Unit here?" I hear Brandon ask.

I turn to see Detective Callahan pinching the bridge of his nose, "Seems this case could be tied to some other cases they are working on," he says, sighing.

He looks at me, "We will type up our reports and send a copy over to you, will that be okay?"

"Yes, Detective, and if you prefer, I can have one of my agents come pick up the file from you. I'm really sorry to encroach on your territory," I start, but he waves his hand in the air to cut me off.

"You are not, Agent Chandler, I just don't like the thought of a serial killer coming into my county. I'm sorry about my abruptness before, cases involving young females always get to me."

"Do either of you know the victim?" I ask.

"No, and I thought I knew just about everyone, since the county isn't really that big out here," Caulder says.

"She looks like someone I would have gone to school with if she grew up here, and I don't know her, so either she just moved to town, or she was visiting someone," Brandon says.

"We will check missing person's and see if anyone reported her," Caulder says, and I nod.

"I'll let you Detectives get back to it," I tell them before walking back to where my team is currently standing and waiting for me.

"I need everyone to look around and document what you see. Declan, could you make a sketch of this area as it is, and Kim, could you please take pictures and video."

I watch as the rest of the team fans out, not knowing what we are looking for, but looking all the same.

After spending an hour looking and documenting, we head back to our car to make the drive back to Largo. Once back in the office, I pull everyone into the conference room.

"Do you believe the female found today is also connected to these other cases?" Mya asks.

"According to Dr. Farrell, she shows the same signs and manner of death, and it's hard not to jump to the conclusion based on that and the area where she was found. What we do know for sure is that we have four victims, in four different counties, brutalized and killed in the same manner, and she could be our fifth victim," I tell them.

"Here are the sketches and pictures from the other scenes that we visited last week," Declan says, laying everything out on the conference table for all of us to see. "While I was doing the sketch at today's scene, I noticed several similarities," he adds.

"I agree, being at two of the scenes and then today, they are very similar," Kim states.

"Looking at these sketches, it seems our killer has a pension for parks with lakes nearby, but shrubs that block the view from the park. I wonder why." I ponder the thought out loud.

'If he is committing the crimes there, no one will be able to see him directly, however it's a good cover for a body dump as well," Frankie voices.

"What are the other similarities?" I ask.

Mya jumps in. "After going through the files, I can tell you our killer has a thing for young females with blond hair and blue eyes. According to the autopsy reports, they were all well-toned which makes me wonder..." she keeps her eyes focused on the paper in front of her.

"I wonder if all these women are joggers, and that's how he finds his victims," she finishes her thought as she continues to look at the reports and the pictures.

"That's a good question," I say, looking at the photos. "We know the first victim was for sure a jogger, her family stated as much when asked why she would be there. We still don't have any identities of the other victims, but let's assume they are all joggers, how does he know which parks to find them? These are all in different counties, where is the unsubs homebase?" I ask.

Everyone is quiet as we ponder those questions.

"Another question is where are the victims' clothes? They don't run around naked, but they aren't at the scene either," Kim adds.

She makes a good point, and I have no answer as I ponder the question in my head. I say out loud, "I'm going to go see Dr. Farrell and see if she can shed any light with the latest victim. Maybe there is something he did differently that will help us. I need the rest of you to continue combing through the files, pictures, and what we saw today. We need to build a profile of this killer. Heath, I need you to check the National Database for missing females that fit these descriptions."

"Sure, Boss, but I thought we were going to wait to see if the counties found anything in their area," he says.

"I was, but something the young Detective said today made me think some of these females may not be from where they were found. It could be they were visiting for one reason or another, and if they were reported missing, it would be from their hometown. The Detectives are looking at their local missing database, we need to search wide," I say before walking out of the conference room.

I know my team will comb through everything, dissecting every piece of the puzzle, but my mind is on Michelle. I saw the devastation in her eyes as she examined the female at the scene. I need to make sure she is okay.

I get in my car and drive to the state building, all the while my mind is on how the killer finds his victims, and what does he do with their clothes and the nipples he cuts off? Why does he cut off their nipples? So many questions and no answers.

When I walk into the state building, I go straight to the elevator, punching the down button. When it opens, I walk in, hitting B for the basement. I wait for the doors to close, while my mind keeps racing over the questions.

When the doors open, I still have no answers, but I do know where I will find Michelle, so I walk straight to the morgue, knowing she will probably still be in the middle of her autopsy. Peeking in through the window of the double door, I see her over the steel table, as she is documenting her findings into a recording.

I push the door open as quietly as I can so as not to disturb her, but I would like to hear what she is saying.

Without even turning around, she turns the recorder off and says, "Hello, Agent Chandler. I have not completed my findings yet."

"That's not why I'm here," I tell her.

She turns around, and I can see the tear streaks on her face.

I open my arms and tell her, "Come here, wife."

She practically races into my arms and silently cries into my chest.

I continue holding her, allowing her to get it all out.

Chapter Ten

MICHELLE

When he opened his arms for me, I didn't stop to think, I just ran into them. I couldn't hold back anymore, and allowed my body to release the cry I had been holding in. Eric continues to hold me until I have no more tears left to cry.

I pull back, looking at his white shirt, now soaked with my tears and smears of mascara. "I'm so sorry," I tell him as I walk over to get a tissue from the counter in the room.

"Don't worry, I have another shirt I can change into. Do you want to talk about it?"

Do I? I ask myself, and without another thought, the words come out of my mouth. "She's very young, younger than the others. I would put her age, late teens, early twenties. She was a virgin, and he brutalized her," I tell him.

I watch as his lips press together knowing he's angry, but not saying anything and allowing me to get it all out.

"The pain this girl must have gone through, I can't imagine," I say, shaking my head, "But he did do something he hadn't with the others."

"Oh, what's that?" Eric asks.

"I found some semen in her anal cavity, and took a swab. I don't know if we will get a DNA match, or if it's too compromised from her body being in the water, but that was something different, and there is another thing," I say, waking over to the body with Eric following me.

"There is this bruise on her temple and the side of her face," I say as I pull her hair back, "None of the other victims showed signs of bruising on their temples."

"Do you know how she got it?"

"There are several different ways, either being punched in the head, or he could have held her head down on something in the ground that could have caused it. I can't be sure," I tell him.

"Can you tell if there are any other differences?" he asks.

"No, everything else seems to be the same MO. Her throat is completely raw, but nothing that points to how he suffocates them to death," I say, sighing.

"Hey," he calls out to me, and I look up at him. "This is not your fault," he tells me.

"If only I found something on the other women, maybe she would still be here," I tell him, feeling the tears pooling again in my eyes.

"You can only find what there is to find. This man is smart, but he already slipped up, and it's only a matter of time before we find him," he tells me before wrapping me up in his arms again and holding me.

"I know, it just hurts to know someone could be so cruel to someone so young," I tell him, keeping the tears at bay.

"I know, but I promise together we will find this man and put him away for a long time. I have the team working on a profile, though we don't have a lot to go on at the moment. We know he likes blondes with blue eyes..."

"That's not true," I cut in. "This victim has green eyes, about the only thing that is the same is the hair color, so maybe he just likes blondes." I tell him.

"Hmmm, that is another difference from the others. We assumed because they all had blue eyes, that was his preference, but you may be right," Eric says.

I can tell he's thinking, but then he shakes his lead, looks down at me and says, "Are you going to be okay?"

"Yeah, I'll be okay," I say, stepping away from him and giving him a small smile.

"I'm sorry that after our relaxing weekend away, this is what we had to come back to," he tells me.

"I know, I wish we could shut out the real world and stay in our little bubble, but unfortunately, that's not reality," I tell him, sighing as I look back at the young woman on my table. "I should finish up here, and once I have the report complete, I'll bring over the file," I tell him.

"Shell," he whispers, and I look up at him. "I love you, and I'm here for you when you need me."

"I know, and I love you too. There are just some things you can't fix, but I'll be okay. We just need to find this monster," I tell him softly.

"And we will, unfortunately we need more time and answers," he tells me before kissing the top of my head and leaving.

"Yeah, and we don't have either right now," I whisper as the door closes.

I pick up my recorder, press the record button, and continue where I left off before Eric walked in.

An hour later, Janine comes in to get the samples of everything I took for testing.

"Can you put a rush on this one for DNA testing?"

"I will flag it as top priority," she tells me before walking out.

I cover the young woman up and put her into cold storage, before going back to my office to transcribe for my reports.

A few hours later, there is a knock on my door, and when I look up, it's Kim holding up a bag of food.

"I brought you some lunch," she says, and as my stomach grumbles. I look at the clock on my computer to see it says it's already two o'clock in the afternoon.

"I didn't realize how late it got," I tell her.

"I figured as much, so I thought I'd grab something and make sure you ate," she says, taking a seat in the chair across from my desk and pulling out a sandwich before handing it to me. Then she pulls one out for herself, and we both take a bite.

Before I know it, my sandwich is gone. Apparently, I was hungrier than I realized.

"Better?" she asks.

"Yeah, thank you," I tell her with a smile.

"No worries. I know how you get with cases," she tells me, waving her hand.

"I know you didn't come down here just to feed me, so what's going on?" I ask her.

"Now, that hurts. Can't a friend come check on her best friend without another motive?"

"Yes, but I can see in your eyes there is something else," I tell her, leaning back in my chair and waiting for her to spill.

She sighs, "That's the downside to having a best friend, they see everything."

"So spill. This wouldn't by chance have something to do with a guy, would it?" I ask her.

I watch as her eyes light up, and she gasps, "How did you know?"

"Kim, I've known you for a long time. I can tell when you are interested in someone, when you've been heartbroken, and when you are completely smitten. Right now, you are smitten, but worried."

"Yeah, and I'm not sure what to do," she says with a sigh.

"Tell me about it," I say more so about my situation with Eric, then her actually telling me about it, but apparently, that's all she needs to hear, because she starts to spill.

"I've been seeing this guy for six months, and I am really invested in him. When we are together, the world makes sense."

"That's great. As long as you are happy, I don't see the problem," I tell her.

"The problem is, there is another guy who thinks he's in love with me, and even though I tell him I'm not interested, he seems to think I will change my mind one day, which makes being honest very diffi-cult."

"I take it these guys know each other?"

"Yeah."

"How does the guy you are with feel about all this?"

"Neither of us want to hide our relationship anymore, but he understands. He doesn't like that his friend is interested in me, but we both know that should his friend find out about us, he could make our lives difficult."

"And you want to know what to do about the friend you are not interested in?" I ask her.

She nods. "I don't want to hurt anyone, but I also don't want to lose the guy I'm with. I do love him, and I'm sure he loves me too."

"He would have to, if he hasn't already told his friend to back off in order to protect you." I lean over the desk, and in a whisper ask, "I take it that something happened this weekend?"

She nods.

"So this has something to do with your co-workers? It would have to be between Declan and Frankie as we both know Heath is gay."

She doesn't say anything, and that's telling enough.

"Want to tell me about it, in detail?"

"I should go back to the office," she says quickly.

"Kim, I'm here to listen whenever you want to talk, and you know I will never tell a soul about anything you tell me."

"I know, but I also don't want to put you in a situation where you have to keep a secret from someone else."

"Who is someone else?" I ask.

"Yep, look at the time, I really should get going," she says.

"Thanks for lunch," I call out as she bolts out of the office.

"You're welcome," she calls back from the hall.

I shake my head. I know one day we will both be honest with each other when the time is right, but these little hints she drops, I know she knows.

It's seven o'clock by the time I'm finished transcribing my reports. I quickly send Eric a text.

> Leaving the office now, be home shortly.

My phone dings with a response,

> Drive safely and see you soon.

I pack up my stuff, grab the file copy for Eric and his team, lock my door, and head for the elevator.

When I walk in the door of my apartment, I'm greeted with the wonderful smell of dinner. God, I'm so lucky this man can cook and loves to cook. I think it's his way of decompressing as jogging is mine.

I will need to make sure to hit the trail tomorrow as it's been a few days since I last jogged.

"What smells so good tonight?" I call out, leaving my bags by the door and walking toward the kitchen.

I find him standing at the stove in sweatpants and a t-shirt.

"I made your favorite. I figured after the day you had, you deserve to have comfort food tonight," he tells me, wrapping me into a hug and kissing my lips.

"I have the most thoughtful husband ever," I tell him when we break the kiss.

"Go change into comfy clothes, and I'll make our plates. I already have the movie cued up that will go perfectly with dinner."

"I love you," I tell him, giving him one more kiss, before walking to the bedroom to change into leggings and a t-shirt.

"I love you more," he calls back.

I can't help the smile that forms on my face. My husband really is the best medicine for a bad day.

I think about my conversation with Kim today and how I want her to be as happy as I am, but I'm not sure how to help her with this situation when I don't have all the details. I can assume she is with Declan, who would be perfect for her, and it's Frankie that is pushing her.

It would make sense, Declan is only a year younger than Kim and I, whereas Frankie is thirty-four and still acts like a child sometimes. Declan is six foot one, with blond hair, blue eyes, and tan skin. Just the type Kim would normally be attracted to. He has a sweet, quiet personality, but I see the protectiveness inside of him.

Of course, I'm only speculating what would make sense to me, and I could be wrong, but something tells me I'm not. If I'm right, I can understand her hesitation and dilemma. Frankie could cause all sorts of issues, especially since there is a no dating policy amongst the team.

It's a policy the team put in place themselves, and she could use that against Frankie, but that means keeping things with Declan completely secret if they want to remain on the same team. Though, there is always the option of one of them requesting a reassignment to another team.

Of course, I see nothing wrong with secret romances, but Eric and I are different from Kim and Declan, and neither would want to leave the team they are currently on, even for the relationship.

It's a situation only they both can work out. I just hope they can find a solution without anyone getting hurt.

I finish getting changed and walk out to the living room, leaving Kim and Declan's situation behind so I can focus on my husband this evening.

Chapter Eleven

ERIC

I watch my wife walk into the living room in her leggings and t-shirt, looking a little more carefree. I know the events of today were overwhelming for her, otherwise she would never have broken down at work like she did.

I made the decision when I left her office that I would ensure she had a relaxing evening with all her comforts, so I came home and made her favorite meal, lasagna. When she wasn't home by five thirty, I checked her phone location and saw she was still at work. I knew she was trying to get her reports completed before she left for the night. I also know that Kim took her lunch at two o'clock this afternoon, which I was grateful for, otherwise she would have forgotten to eat again.

She sits down next to me on the couch, and I pass her the plate I made. I hit play on her favorite movie, The Notebook, and settle in with my plate.

I hear her moan, when she takes the first bite, and I smile. We finish eating our meal, and I take everything to the kitchen to clean-up, while she continues watching the movie. When it's time I pass her the tissue box, she always cries at the end, but this time, I know she's crying about everything, and I let her, while holding her.

When she's finished, I take her to bed, tuck her in against me and listen as her breathing evens out and she falls fast asleep.

In the morning, when we both wake, I start the shower, allowing the water to warm up, before going to make the coffee, but when I get to the kitchen, I see her already there.

"Thought I would make coffee this morning while you were getting the shower ready," she says with a smile.

"You know you didn't have to do that," I tell her.

"I know, but you took such good care of me last night, I want to return the favor this morning. How about we go get that shower, and I show you how thankful I am," she says with a naughty grin on her face.

"Ahh, Mrs. Chandler, what do you have in mind?" I ask her with a smirk.

"Why don't you come find out," she says, walking down the hall, looking over her shoulder, and beckoning me with her finger.

I can't help the swelling of my cock as I watch her hips sway or the hungry look in her eyes.

I follow her into the shower, grabbing her by the back of the neck and kissing her deeply.

She pushes me back against the shower wall, then drops down to her knees. Fuck she looks so gorgeous when she takes my cock into her mouth and stares up at me with her beautiful green eyes.

She swirls her tongue around the head of my cock, lapping up the pre-cum from the tip. Then she slides her tongue from the base of my shaft up before taking the whole thing back in her mouth and sucking.

"Oh, you do that so fucking good," I tell her in a growl.

She moans, causing the vibration to go through me and up my spine, then she takes me deeper, hitting the back of her throat. I about come undone when she starts to gag.

I lift her hair, so I can watch her mouth as she relaxes her throat more and continues to take me deeper.

"Damn, baby, feels so fucking good," I say, closing my eyes, and enjoying the feeling of her warm mouth wrapped around my cock, while she sucks me so fucking good.

She grabs onto my thighs, taking one hand up and cupping my balls. I can't help taking over and thrust into her as I fuck her mouth. Every time she gags, I want to go deeper.

I look down and see saliva dripping from her mouth onto my cock, as her eyes peer up at me with love and desire. I continue staring at her as she continues to take my cock, until I feel my spine tingle and my balls tighten up.

"I'm going to come down your throat, and you are going to take it all," I tell her, and she nods her head, letting me know she's ready, as I come hard.

When I look down at her, I see some of my cum dribbling down the side of her mouth, but she sucks my cock until it's soft, releasing it like a lollipop, then wipes her mouth.

I lift her up, placing her against the shower wall and tell her, "Now it's your turn, baby," before eating her soaking wet pussy.

"OH, God, Eric, OH..." she calls out.

I moan, enjoying the taste of her on my tongue, then I suck on her clit, biting down with enough pressure causing her to explode, and I lap all her juices up, before sitting her feet back on the shower floor and washing her up.

"I love these mornings with you," she says as she lathers my body with soap.

"I do too, and I hope we are still doing this when we are eighty," I tell her with a smile.

She laughs, "I hope so too."

We finish washing up, we get out of the shower, and get dressed for the day. There is a lot of work that needs to be done if we are going to find this killer.

I get to the office and find Detective Burton waiting by the elevators for me.

"Detective Burton, what can I do for you today?"

"I just came by to check and see if you have any more news about the cases, well more specifically mine," he says, looking tired.

"Why don't you come upstairs, and we can talk," I tell him as the elevator door opens, and I fob us to the fourth floor.

"Thank you, I appreciate it," he tells me.

When we get off the elevator, I unlock the door to our offices and usher him inside.

"Why don't you go into the conference room where we can talk, and I can show you what we know so far," I tell him, pointing toward the conference room.

I walk into my office to grab a couple of files, then head into the conference room. I find Detective Burton looking at the sketches we have on the board.

"Is this Pritchard County?" he asks, pointing to the latest sketch from yesterday.

"Have you been there before?"

"Absolutely. I was just there this past weekend," he says before shaking his head. "Did you find a body there?"

"Yes, we did. What were you doing there?"

"My granddaughter does travel soccer, and there was a tournament there this past weekend. As part of her wind down, we always get some food, sit by a lake, eat and relax before heading home. Sometimes she will jog a few laps if she's really keyed up from the game," he offers up.

"How did she do this weekend?"

"Her team won both games on Saturday. On Sunday, they won the first one, but lost by a point in the second, and finished the tournament off at number two," he says with a smile .

I can tell he loves his granddaughter.

"I didn't get to see Sunday's game, I was called back to Chatam for a robbery/homicide, but her mom kept me informed through text and video."

"How old is your granddaughter?"

"She's seventeen and will be a senior starting in the fall. She and her parents have been deciding on which colleges to visit this summer. Of course they would prefer she stay close to home, since she is their only child, but she's ready to spread her wings," he says with a chuckle.

I can't help the chuckle that leaves my mouth as I nod in understanding.

Before either of us can say anything more, Detective Burton's phone rings. He looks down at the caller ID and says, "I need to take this, sorry."

I wave my hand in understanding.

"James, what's going on?"

"How long? Did you try to call?"

"I'll be right there," he says as he hangs up.

"I'm sorry, Agent Chandler, I need to go, apparently my granddaughter has not been home in a couple of days, and her cell phone is off."

"I hope everything is okay?"

"I'm sure it is, could just be miscommunication," he says, but not sounding convinced.

"If you need help, let me know."

"Thanks, appreciate it," he says, heading for the elevators quickly.

"Hey, was that Detective Burton?"

"Yeah, he got a call about his granddaughter potentially missing," I say, a little worried. "I told him if he needed our help, to let us know," I add.

The team nods, as they continue to drop their gear, and make their way into the conference room.

I pass them the latest autopsy report from Michelle on our current victim. She brought it home last night and left it for me on the table by the door. I haven't had the opportunity to read it yet, but I know enough from what Michelle told me yesterday.

"Heath, did you find anything in the national database?"

"Boss, there are hundreds of missing females that match these descriptions. I'm going to need more in order to narrow it down any further," he tells me.

"Did you focus solely on women in the state of Maine?" I ask.

"Yes, that's how I went from thousands to hundreds, as well as reducing down to eye color of only blue-and green-eyed blondes. Still left with hundreds."

"Wow, that's a lot of missing females," Mya says, and everyone nods in agreement.

"Unfortunately, we have nothing more to go on, so we can only hope the local counties are able to find a match," I say as my phone pings with an incoming text.

I shake my head, and sigh. "Mya, can you go down and bring Detective Smith up. He says he has something for us."

"Great," she mumbles, while leaving the conference room and heading for the elevator.

Mya returns with a very energetic Detective on her heels.

"Special Agent Chandler, I think I found the victim," he says enthusiastically without any greeting.

I hold out my hand for his folder, and he hands it to me. I open the file and see the name of Amanda Toliver, age twenty-five, missing for four weeks now.

"Have you spoken with the person who reported her missing?"

"No, sir, not yet. I'm not sure how to go about telling them we may have found her body," he says with a sadness in his tone.

"Well, there is no time like the present. Maybe they will have something of hers we can use for DNA testing to see if we have a match. This is a good start, Detective, but there is still so much more to do. I will come with you, and help where I can," I tell him.

"I would appreciate it, Sir. I know this is important, and I don't want to mess it up," he admits, and I can admire that he really wants to learn.

"There may be some hope for you yet, Detective," I say as I walk out of the conference room, with Detective Smith following me to the elevators.

I follow behind Detective Smith all the way to Lorn County and to the address of the person who reported the young woman missing. When we get there, I notice it's a law firm.

Detective Smith and I walk in and we are immediately greeted by a receptionist.

"Can I help you, Gentlemen?" she asks.

"We need to speak to Julian Gunter," Detective Smith tells her.

"Do you have an appointment?" she asks.

"No. I'm Detective Smith with the Lorn County Police Department, and this is Special Agent Chandler of the FBI Behavioral Unit," he informs her, and I watch as her mouth parts a little bit.

"One second, please," she says as she gets up from the desk, walks down the little hallway and knocks on a door before opening it.

I can hear some murmuring of voices, but they are speaking so softly I can't make out words or tone.

The receptionist comes back with a female dressed in a business suit following behind her. She looks to be five two if you take the heels off, dark brown shoulder length hair, and brown eyes that look concerned right now.

"I'm Julian Gunter, how can I help you Gentlemen?" she asks.

"You filed a missing person's report, and we'd like to ask you some questions," Detective Smith says.

"Yes, please come back to my office," she tells us, then looks at her receptionist and says, "Hold all my calls."

"Yes, ma'am."

We are led into a nicely furnished office with a small conference table, and that is where we are asked to sit.

"Is this about Amanda? Have you found her?"

"We are not sure, and could use some more information," I say, before Detective Smith can utter a word.

"Okay, sure," she says.

"Can you tell us why you think Amanda is missing and who she is to you?" I ask.

"Amanda is my paralegal. I hired her two years ago when she moved here. Her parents had passed away, she has no siblings, and nothing to keep her in her hometown, so she was driving with no particular place in mind, came into our town and fell in love with it. The only issue is she had no job, but she had a paralegal degree. She came in looking for work as a paralegal, at the time, I already had a paralegal, so I hired her as my receptionist. Before long, she was doing her job and helping the paralegal, showing me she knew what she was doing." She takes a deep breath.

"A year ago, Denise retired, and I moved Amanda into the paralegal role. We became best friends in the last two years, so I found it odd when she didn't show up for work that Monday. We had a big case we were working on for trial, and it was not like her not to call and let me know where she was at. I tried calling her cell, but it immediately went straight to voicemail, letting me know it was turned off. I drove over to her apartment, knocked on the door, no response. I have an extra key to her place, so I went in and looked around. Everything was in its place, but no Amanda," she tells us.

"You have a key to her place?" I ask.

She nods.

"Would it be possible for us to go over there to get something with her DNA on it?" I ask.

"If you think it will help, absolutely. It's been four weeks, and I know something has happened, she would not show up to work or call," she tells us as her voice cracks.

"Can you tell us what she liked to do when she wasn't working?" I ask.

"She and I would go to the park and jog the path to help decompress, especially before we would go into a courtroom. That was how we bonded, she had asked about a good place to go run, and I told her where I usually go." She chuckles.

"I didn't really expect her to show up, people say they like to run, but usually they don't, they just want to impress someone, but not her. Amanda loved to run, and after that first day, we became running partners, but sometimes, she would go out there twice a day to clear her head. It always made her feel good to work through problems by running."

"I understand, I have a few agents who do the same," I admit, thinking about Kim, Heath, and Michelle.

I can see Detective Smith looking at me, but I continue looking at Ms. Gunter when I ask, "Would you mind taking us over to Amanda's place and letting us in?"

"Sure, let me grab her keys. She only lives about five blocks away, so if you don't mind the walk, we can walk over there."

"We don't mind at all," I tell her, answering for both the Detective and myself. I can tell she is very worried and needs to move her legs.

Stepping into the apartment, I immediately see how clean and organized everything is. "Amanda liked control, didn't she?" I ask.

"She did. She hated chaos, everything had to be in its place. I used to laugh at her, and tell her whenever she started dating again, she wouldn't be able to control that. She said it would be awhile before that ever happened, she wanted a career first," she says, sounding very emotional.

Detective Smith comes out of the bathroom with a toothbrush in one evidence bag, and hair that I assume he took from her hairbrush, in another bag.

"We will get these tested and placed in the database. If we find her, I promise we will let you know," I tell her.

"I would greatly appreciate that, and until then, I'm going to continue to pray she is alive and was in an accident, maybe has amnesia somewhere."

I give her an encouraging nod, because there is nothing wrong with praying for a better outcome, but my gut is screaming we found our second victim.

When Detective Smith and I leave Ms. Gunter to lock up the apartment, he looks at me and says, "I really do have a lot to learn."

"It comes with experience," I tell him.

"The way you asked her questions, without telling her that we may have found Amanda was amazing. I never even thought to engage in conversational questioning."

"Like I said, it comes with experience. There will be plenty of trial and error, but you are young, and I believe you will do well."

"Thank you. Being able to watch and listen to you really helped me understand a little bit more of what I need to work on. I appreciate the help, Special Agent."

"It's all about the victims, never forget that," I tell him as I take the evidence and get in my car to drive back to Largo.

Chapter Twelve

MICHELLE

Eric brought me items to have the lab do DNA testing and run them against the current victims still in the morgue. I've sent the samples to the lab, and all we can do is wait and see if we get a DNA match.

My phone pings with a group text from Kim.

> **Heath: You know I'm in. Don't leave me this time, sis.**

> **Kim: Make sure you are ready on time.** ⊠

I can't help the laugh that slips out. Heath is still chasing the dream of hope in finding his mister perfect. I really do hope he finds him one day.

The next text surprises me.

> **Frankie: I'll go, could be fun.**

Frankie has never shown any interest in running with us, but I'm not surprised by the next text.

> **Declan: I'm in.**

I knew he was protective, and there is no way he would allow Frankie to hover over Kim, if they are indeed in a relationship as I suspect they are.

> **Eric: Have fun everyone, be safe, and stay together. No injuries please, we still have work to do.**

I laugh out loud. Only Eric can make everything about work in the end. I know he'll go home and make us something good for dinner, of course I'm looking forward to the shower we will both have when I get home from running before we eat.

I think about how he took care of me last night, making my favorite meal of lasagna, putting on my favorite movie, and allowing me to cry, before tucking me into bed. Of course, I thanked him very well this morning while we were in the shower. I love when I drive him crazy and cause him to lose control. It turns me on more than his heated looks.

Ping.

I place my phone down, knowing I only have forty-five minutes to complete this paperwork, change, and drive to the park.

I look at the clock as I file the last document, seeing that it's fifteen minutes to five. I am right on time. I quickly change into my running gear, grabbing my stuff, locking up the office, and heading for the elevator.

"Janine, I'm heading out for a run. I'll see you tomorrow," I call out to her.

"Okay, Doctor, have a nice night," she calls back.

I get in the elevator, making my way up to the parking lot.

I pull in the parking lot of the park at the same time Kim and Heath pull in.

Heath gets out of the car, and I hear him say, "All I'm saying is it wouldn't hurt for you to get a more colorful outfit and flaunt your assets. I'm trying to help you."

"Did it ever occur to you that maybe I don't need help with my attire," she says, walking over to me as her phone rings.

I watch as she looks down to see who is calling, then pushes decline. She looks up at me, and I give her a questioning look, but she shrugs her shoulders and begins stretching.

"Are you seeing someone?" Heath asks, shocked and hurt that she hadn't told him.

She sighs, "That's not what I said. I shouldn't have to change who I am for someone."

"That's very true. No one would appreciate someone who couldn't be themselves," Frankie says, walking up with Declan.

We all begin to stretch, when I look at Heath and see him contemplating what Frankie said.

"As weird as it is to hear coming from Frankie, he is right," I say. "When you are yourself, you are bound to find the right one for you."

Heath sighs, "I know, but no one ever notices the smart, quiet guy."

We all laugh, "Heath, you are anything but quiet," I tell him, "And there is nothing wrong with being a smart guy. Everyone wants a smart partner, just don't be a smartass."

"Hunny buns, my ass always looks smart, especially in these shorts," he says, modeling for us all, causing laughing fits all around.

"I would have to agree," a guy standing by his car, stretching says. He looks to be around Heath's age, maybe a year or two older, dark wavy hair, and deep chocolate brown eyes. He's wearing black running pants, and a tight gray t-shirt.

He walks over to our group and says, "Hi, I'm Chris."

"I...umm...I...." Heath stutters.

"Hi, I'm Kim, and this stuttering fool is Heath."

"I would love a running partner, are you interested?" Chris asks Heath.

Heath is so smitten by Chris' looks, he can only nod and follow Chris to the jogging path.

"Hopefully he is able to form a complete and coherent sentence," I say with a chuckle. "Ready?" I ask the rest of the group.

Nods go around, and we make our way to the trail, with Kim and I in the lead. Half an hour into the run, it seems the guys have fallen back.

"I guess they aren't in as much shape as they thought they were," I say, giggling.

Kim looks back over her shoulder, then she looks at me and giggles too, "Guess not."

"I hope Heath is okay and enjoying his time," I say, chewing on my bottom lip, concern filling me for Heath.

"Oh, I'd say he is doing just fine," Kim responds, nodding her head at the bench to our right, where Heath and Chris are currently chatting and laughing about something. They both look relaxed and happy.

"I hope this leads to something good for him," I say.

"Me too. He deserves to be happy," she says.

"And so do you," I tell her.

Kim sighs deeply, "I know, but that means making some big decisions."

"Nothing needs to be decided right now, just enjoy what you have, and who knows, maybe things will work out on their own without you having to make any big decisions," I tell her.

"Hmm, maybe," she says, though not sounding convinced.

I say nothing more as we continue making our laps. In the end, it will be her decision on how she handles the things in her life.

I will always be here to support her, I just hope that doesn't mean having to support her while she's in DC again. I really do enjoy seeing her all the time. Sometimes it feels like we are back in college, trading secrets in our dorm room.

Once we are done, she and I go back to the parking lot to do our cool down, while we wait for the guys to show up.

"Heath, I would like to see you again, how about dinner?" I hear Chris ask.

"I'd like that," Heath says.

At least he finally found his voice, even if it sounds a bit uneven at the moment.

"Great, will an hour and a half be enough time for you to get ready?"

"You mean tonight?" Heath asks, shock evident in his voice.

"Unless you have other plans?" Chris asks.

"No, I don't. Hour and a half should be enough time."

"Great, just text me your address, and I'll pick you up," he says, as he grabs Heath's phone, inputting his number. I watch as he presses send on a text. "Now I have your number, and I look forward to hearing from you soon."

Chris passes Heath back his phone, then starts to walk toward his car, when he stops and turns, "Oh, and Heath."

"Yes?"

"It's casual," he says, before turning back and going to his car.

"You have a date," Kim says with a smile.

"I have a date," Heath says, sounding stunned.

"Why do you sound so surprised?" I ask him.

"I mean, we had a great conversation, and I thought everything went well. I just didn't expect him to ask me out for dinner so quickly. Oh my God, what am I going to wear?" he asks with a screech.

"Calm down, Diva, the man said casual," Kim tells him.

"Casual slacks or casual jeans? And before you ask, yes there is a difference," he says as he starts to hyperventilate.

"Heath, calm down. It's going to be fine, no need to get yourself all worked up. Go with the slacks, but most importantly, be yourself and have a good time," I tell him.

"If I had all day to prepare, I'd be okay, but I only have a," looking down at his watch, "I have an hour and twenty minutes to get home, shower, and find something casual to wear. What the hell was I thinking?"

"Good thing you only live ten minutes away from here, now calm down. If you had all day to prepare you would be going out of your mind. He did this to take the pressure of waiting all day off the table.

You're going to have a wonderful meal and spend time getting to know a hottie," Kim tells him.

"He is hot," he says, looking down at his watch, "Shit, come on, we have to go. I'm running out of time," Heath says dramatically racing over to Kim's car.

"Hey, Heath," I call out.

"What?"

"How about you start by texting him your address, so he knows you're serious about dinner, then take a deep breath, and enjoy yourself," I call out to him.

"Address, right," he says, pulling up his phone and quickly sending off the text. "Come on, Kimmy, by the time I get home, I'll only have an hour to get to perfection," he whines.

She and I both laugh, and she follows him to her car, saying, "I thought you were already perfection?"

"Girl, do you think I wake up looking this good?"

"To hear you talk, yes," she tells him seriously.

"Pfff, I do, but to look extra good, I need help. Maybe I should give you some pointers," he says as he gets into the car, closing the door.

Declan and Frankie make it to the parking lot as Kim and Heath pull away.

"They are leaving already?" Frankie asks breathlessly.

"Yeah, Heath has a dinner date tonight, and Kim has to get him home so he can prepare," I say, laughing and shaking my head.

"Good for him," Declan says. "I need to get home and get a shower after that run. I guess there really is a difference between running on a treadmill and actually running," he adds.

"I agree," Frankie said, trying to get his breathing under control from the run.

"There most certainly is, but don't worry, if you both keep it up, eventually you won't fall behind," I tell him with a smile before heading to my vehicle. I'm ready to get home to Eric.

Chapter Thirteen

UNKNOWN

The demon is trying to overpower me, but I refuse to allow him to hurt another person. I can't be the reason another girl is brutalized.

You know you like it, why are you fighting it?

"Because it's wrong, what you make us do is wrong," I say through gritted teeth.

Wrong, right, what does it matter when it all feels so good.

"I can't listen to you anymore. I need to find a way to get you out of my head," I say, beating the side of my head with my fist.

That will never happen. You need me as much as I need you."

"I don't need you," I tell the demon.

Have you forgotten who saved you? If it wasn't for me, you would still be whimpering on the floor.

"I have not forgotten," I whisper.

They did this to us, we are just reacting to the urges they set in motion.

"We can stop this, though," I say.

No, it's too late for all that, and oh look, here's a perfect one right now.

I didn't realize we had left the safety of our room, and now we are in a park, following the blond running around the park.

"When did we leave?" I whisper.

I told you I'm stronger than you.

I have to find a way to stop this, there must be a way, but the demon just laughs inside me and then says, good luck with that, until then, I'll enjoy the fruits.

Before he could do anything more, the female joins up with a male on the jogging path, and I sigh with relief.

"You may be stronger than me for now, but God will find a way to protect the innocent," I whisper.

Your God hasn't done such a great job so far, has he? He didn't protect you, and he hasn't protected them.

Unfortunately, I can't argue with him, but today, God is answering my prayers.

It's fine, there's someone else I want anyways. We need to find Her.

"We can't..." I start.

We can and we will.

Chapter Fourteen

Eric

Last night when Michelle came home from her run in the park, she was full of smiles. Seems Heath found himself a date at the park and was a bit of a girl about it all. I didn't understand everything she was saying, but the fact that she was smiling made me happy.

I'm sitting in my office this morning, waiting for the team to show up, trying to figure out what we are missing with this case. How can this killer go unnoticed, doing the things he is doing to these women? How are they not fighting back?

There are so many questions with these cases, and nothing to point to any answers. What is he doing with their clothes? Cell phones? Why is he leaving them in the lake?

So many questions, but the main one is why don't we know who they all are?

"Hey, boss," Kim says, peeking into my office.

"Good morning, Kim, what's going on?"

"Detective Burton was down in the lobby, asking to see you. I brought him up."

"Send him in," I tell her.

"Sorry to intrude, Special Agent," he says as he walks in with his shoulders slumped and his hair unkempt. He doesn't look like he slept at all last night.

"Call me Eric, and it's no intrusion. Did you find your granddaughter?" I ask, knowing he wouldn't look like this if they had.

"No, and that's why I'm here. I'd like to see the body you found in Pritchard County. I need to make sure it's not her. My daughter-in-law is beside herself with worry, and my son is trying to be strong for her, but I can tell he's barely holding it together. To be honest, I'm barely holding it together."

"I can call Dr. Farrell and see if she will allow us to come view the body," I tell him, picking up the desk phone.

"State of Maine Morgue, this is Dr. Farrell," she answers sweetly.

I hate that I'm about to dim her day. "Dr. Farrell, this is Special Agent Chandler, is it possible to bring a Detective by to look at the body of the Jane Doe brought in from Pritchard County?"

"Sure. I'll have the body ready for viewing by the time you get here."

"Thank you. We will be there shortly."

I hang up the phone and look at Detective Burton, "She will have everything ready for us by the time we get there. Are you sure you want to do this?"

"Am I sure? No. Do I need to do this? Yes, so I might as well get it over with."

"Okay, then I will drive," I tell him.

We leave my office, and I look at Kim. "I'm taking Detective Burton to see Dr. Farrell."

She nods, not needing to say anything.

I drive us to the state building, and we get out of the car.

"I've never been here before," he says softly.

"I understand. There's not much reason for any of you all to come," I reply, opening the door for us and leading him to the elevator.

Stepping in, I hit the basement floor. When the doors open, I see Michelle standing outside the morgue doors, waiting for us.

"Special Agent Chandler," she says with a nod.

"Dr. Farrell, this is Detective Burton," I introduce her.

"Detective Burton, nice to put a name to the voice," she says, shaking his hand.

"You too, Doctor, just wish it wasn't under these circumstances," he says.

"I'm sorry, but you're from Chatam County, correct?" she says, looking a bit confused.

"He's not here on official business. He's here to see if he can identify the victim from Pritchard County," I tell her.

"Oh," she says, sounding shocked before she recovers and gets back in business mode. "Okay, well if you are ready, then please follow me," she says solemnly.

Michelle leads us into the morgue, where she has the female on the metal table with a sheet covering her.

"Are you ready, Detective?" She asks, and after a brief moment he nods.

She pulls the sheet down to the victim's neck, so he is able to see her face.

I watch as his body slumps, and he sighs deeply.

"Do you know her, Detective Burton?" I ask.

"Yes, I do, but that is not my granddaughter. It's one of her teammates, Krista something. I'm sorry I don't know her last name, but I'm sure I can find out from my daughter-in-law. She has the whole team roster."

"That would be helpful, thank you," I tell him, nodding to Michelle to cover up the victim.

"Thank you, Dr. Farrell," he says, after she puts the young woman back in cold storage.

"It's not a problem, and I'm glad she is not your granddaughter, but she is someone else's."

He nods. "Give me one second, and I'll have the name for you," pulling his phone out of his pocket to call his son, I would assume.

"What's going on?" Michelle asks in a whisper.

"His granddaughter was in Pritchard for a traveling soccer tournament, and never came home," I relay to her.

"Oh, that poor family. How did he know we had a body here?"

"He came to the office yesterday for an update on the case. He saw the picture of the park, told me what county it was and bottom line, when I questioned him, he told me about the tournament. I had mentioned we found another female there, then he received a call that his granddaughter had not come home. This morning, he showed up saying he needed to see our Jane Doe to rule out his granddaughter."

"Oh, I hope they find her," Michelle whispers, biting on her lower lip while looking toward the door where the Detective is at on the phone.

"Me too," I admit quietly.

I watch as the Detective hangs up the phone and comes back through the double doors.

"Her name is Krista Thompson, she's seventeen years old," he chokes out. "She lives is Brewer County, about twenty-five miles from Chatam County," he says.

I look over at Michelle and tell her, "I will get a hold of Brewer County and see if they can send someone out to the family."

"I'll go," Detective Burton says. "I have a friend over in the county, and I will have him go with me to break the news. What do you need Doctor, in order to release?"

"DNA helps, but if the parents are willing to come and identify her themselves, then I can release her to their funeral home of choice," she tells him.

"I will escort them myself when they are ready. I will call you first," he tells her, and she nods in agreement.

"Let me get you back to the building and your car, Detective. Thank you so much, Dr. Farrell," I say to her.

"You are both welcome, and Detective," she calls out. I watch as he turns back to face her, "I'll be praying that your granddaughter is found safe."

"I appreciate that, thank you, Doctor, I'll let her parents know," he tells her before turning back for the door.

I take the Detective back to the parking lot and watch as he gets in his car. I don't envy the task that he is about to do.

I pull my cell phone out of my pocket and call Michelle.

"Hey," she answers.

"Hi, how are you holding up?"

"It's nice to potentially have an identity of the victim, but I'm upset that she was only seventeen, and to be honest, I'm not looking forward to the family coming and identifying her even though I know it needs to be done."

"I know, babe, but you are strong, and you will ensure the family gets what they need."

"Yeah, I will," she says with a sigh.

"I love you," I tell her.

"I love you too," she says, and I can hear a little smile in her voice. "Now, go find out who these other two victims are. Hopefully we will receive the DNA results soon on the other female, and that will tell us for sure who she is. I asked for a rush, but all I can do is wait."

"Yes, ma'am. We are working on it, but now, knowing they could be from any county and not just the county where they were found, makes the job a little more difficult, but we will keep looking. I'll see you at home tonight," I tell her softly.

"I'm not sure what time I'll be home, but I'll see you when I get there."

"Okay, talk to you later," I tell her before hanging up.

I pocket my phone and walk into the building. We need answers, and we need to find this killer before someone else gets hurt.

Chapter Fifteen

MICHELLE

I hang up the phone, loving Eric even more for calling and checking up on me.

Watching the detective leave here was heartbreaking. Not only is he worried about his granddaughter, and rightfully so, but now he must go and tell another family that their child is no longer coming home.

I didn't lie to Eric when I told him I wasn't looking forward to the family coming. I know how difficult and unbelievable this all seems to them. In their mind, there is no way this is their loved one, but when they are faced with seeing the face of the one they know lying here, they either completely lose it or go straight into denial.

I decide to start on the transport paperwork, leaving the name and funeral home blank, as well as the date. It's all busy work to keep my nerves in check while I wait for the phone call that will inevitably come.

I finish the paperwork with as much information as I have, then proceed to go into the morgue and scrub everything, even though it was already scrubbed down last night. I need to keep my hands busy, my body moving, otherwise I will work myself up into a frenzy.

It's after lunch, and I have been unable to eat. My stomach is in knots for what is still to come, when the phone rings.

"State of Maine Morgue, this is Dr. Farrell," I answer, already knowing who will be on the other end.

"Dr. Farrell, it's Detective Burton, the parents would like to come identify the young woman," he tells me.

"I will be here waiting, Detective," I respond, and he hangs up.

Neither of us sound happy about the situation in which we find ourselves.

I send Eric a text.

> **Parents are on their way with the Detective.**

My phone pings with a reply.

> **I'll be over there shortly.**

I knew he would want to be here, not only to make sure I'm okay, but to also talk with the parents and see what they can tell him about the young woman.

Within twenty minutes, Eric shows up. I'm currently in the morgue, getting the young lady out and ready for viewing again.

"Hey," he says quietly, when he comes in.

"Hi," I reply back.

"I know this is hard for you, but everything will be okay," he says, pulling me into a hug.

"I know," I say with a sigh, even with the headache brewing behind my eyes.

"I'll stand over here in the corner. They will all be focused on the table, that they will not notice me, and that's how it should be. Once they confirm her identity, then I will make myself known to the room," he tells me, and I nod.

"I better get in the hall, they should all be here soon," I tell him.

He leans his head down and gives me a soft kiss, then says, "It will be okay. I'm here with you."

I nod, giving him one last hug for strength, then allow him to walk over to the corner, while I walk out into the hallway to wait.

A few minutes later, the elevator doors open and out walks Detective Burton with a blond-haired woman, a tall man with blond hair, and a priest.

The woman is leaning into her husband's side, and I can see she has been crying. He looks stoic, almost like this is a nightmare for him.

The priest casually follows behind them.

"Dr. Farrell, this is Mr. and Mrs. Thompson and Father Mullen. They would like the priest to perform the blessing if this is, in fact, their daughter," Detective Burton informs me.

I nod, "That's perfectly fine. Are you ready?" I ask, looking straight at the mother.

She shakes her head, and I understand completely.

"It's fine, you take as long as you need to," I tell her with a small smile.

"Come on, Layla, we should get this over with," her husband tells her, looking very uncomfortable.

"Okay," she whimpers out.

I lead them into the morgue, and straight to the table. I pull the sheet back on the victim to uncover her face.

"Oh my God, my baby," Mrs. Thompson calls out as she breaks down.

I watch as her husband starts to cry, while holding his wife, and I have to look away. I notice the detective moved over to where Eric is standing.

"I blessed this young woman the other day," I hear the priest say.

"What?" the mother asks.

"Father Callahan and I found this young woman in the lake. I tried hard to bring her back, but she was already gone. Father Callahan and I recited the after-death prayer over this young woman as we waited for the police to come. I'm sorry, I was not aware she was your daughter," he tells them.

"You found her?" Mr. Thompson asks.

"Yes, I'm very sorry I couldn't save her, but she is with God now," the priest says, and though I know he means well, that is not what any parent wants to hear.

"This is your daughter, then?" I ask, jumping in before things are said that can't be taken back.

"Yes, this is our Krista," Mrs. Thompson says.

"Do you have a specific funeral home in mind that you would like us to have her transported to?" I ask.

"On the drive here, I was going over funeral homes for the in case, and I really liked the reviews on McKinney's Funeral Home," Mr. Thompson says.

"I will make the arrangements with them," I tell them.

"Father, would you preside over the service?" Mrs. Thompson asks the priest.

"I would be honored to. We can look at the church calendar and see what day works for you," he tells them both.

He steps back as Eric and Detective Burton walk over from the corner.

"Mr. and Mrs. Thompson, please forgive me during this time, but I am Special Agent Chandler from the Behavioral Unit in Maine, would you mind answering a few questions?"

They both nod, and he walks them out into the hall. I go to cover the girl up, but the priest stops me and asks, "May I say a few more prayers over her body?"

"Sure, Father, let me know when you are finished," I say softly.

I step over to the side, and watch as he silently prayers, touching each one of his rosary beads. When he is done praying, he leaves the sign of the cross on the top of her forehead, then nods at me that he is finished.

I cover the young girl back up and place her back in cold storage before I prep her for transport.

I walk back over to the priest and say, "Thank you, Father, for coming, I know it gave the parents some peace to have you here."

"I don't know about that. I feel like I am the reason she is here. I found her, but I was unable to save her," he says solemnly.

"Father, in my line of work, I've come to realize not everyone can be saved. You tried, but it was too late. She was already gone, probably hours before you found her. Please don't blame yourself. You save people every day, but you know as well as I do, everything is in God's timing," I tell him as I lightly touch his arm.

He looks down where my hand is, taps my hand with his other, before saying, "That is very true, child. Everything is in his timing," he smiles a little, then I remove my hand from his arm.

He follows me out into the hallway, where everyone is gathered. They all turn to me and Father Mullen.

"I will call the funeral home and make the arrangements. They will call you when they have received her. Do you have any questions of me?"

"Do you know how she was killed?" Mrs. Thompson asks.

I look over at Eric and the Detective. Eric nods, so I turn back to the parents.

"She was suffocated, though I have not determined exactly how that happened yet."

Before they could ask any other questions, Detective Burton says, "Let me drive you back home now."

They both nod, "Thank you Dr. Farrell," Mrs. Thompson says.

"Yes, thank you Doctor," Mr. Thompson echoes his wife, before they both head to the elevator, holding onto each other like lifelines.

I really hope they are able to sustain their marriage after losing a child. So many marriages end with the loss of a child as both parents grieve separately, instead of together. Sometimes, one is unable to let go of the grief when the other parent is ready to move on. I just pray that isn't them.

"Are you okay?" Eric asks.

"Yeah, now I need to call the funeral home and see when they can receive Krista before I get her prepped."

"Would you like for me to stay?"

"That's very sweet, but no, you have your own work that needs to be done. I'll be okay," I tell him with a small smile.

"Alright, then I'll see you at home. How about I run you a hot bath tonight?"

"That sounds great," I say with a sigh.

"Okay, finish up here, and I will have everything ready for you at home," he tells me.

I look at my watch and see it's already after five o'clock.

"Wow, I can't believe it's that late already. Give me an hour, and I should be home. I just need to put the new information in the paperwork and make the call."

"Take your time, no need to rush. I'll be waiting," he says with a smile, and I can't help melting.

I watch as he leaves up the elevator, and I go back to my office, hoping someone is still at the funeral home. I also pull up the paper and put Krista's name in the documents as well as the name of the funeral home.

"McKinney's Funeral Home, this is Jack, can I help you?"

"Hi, Jack, this is Dr. Farrell with the State of Maine Morgue. I have a young woman whose parents would like to use your funeral home to receive their daughter."

"Absolutely, Dr. Farrell. What is the deceased's name?"

"Krista Thompson. I also informed the parents that you would be in touch with them once you receive her."

"Yes, most definitely. Would you like to transport her here, or for us to come and transport?"

"We can transport her, will tomorrow morning be okay?"

"Yes, Dr. Farrell, that would be perfect. I will be here to receive the young lady."

"Thank you so much. Have a good evening," I tell him before hanging up.

I print out the documents, leave them on my desk, shutdown my computer, then grab my things, and lock up the office.

Thoughts of a hot bath race through my mind. I can feel the tension in my body and know this is exactly what I need to relieve the pressure I have felt all day.

Chapter Sixteen

Eric

I get home, checking the time and know I have a little while before I need to run the bath for Michelle. I could see the tension and feel the worry pouring off of her when I walked into the morgue. She handled herself like the true professional that she is.

It didn't take long for Detective Burton to notice me standing in the corner as soon as he walked in.

I was completely shocked when Father Mullen walked in with Detective Burton and the parents. Though, I think the parents were more shocked to find out that it was their priest who found the girl.

I sit on the couch thinking back on the conversation that I had with the parents in the hallway.

"I'm so sorry for your loss. I have just a few questions. Can you tell me how old your daughter is?"

"She just turned eighteen last week," Mrs. Thompson says through her tears.

"We planned to have a surprise party for her this weekend, since she had a soccer tournament this past weekend," Mr. Thompson says.

"Was she a jogger?"

"Yes. She loved to run after the games to help bring her adrenaline down. She told us she would get in a quick run at the park, then she was going to meet up with a couple of girls from the team, and they planned on checking out a college for a couple of days before coming home," Mrs. Thompson says.

"Did you try to call her?"

"Yes, but her phone went straight to voicemail, so I assumed she forgot her charger, and she would call and check in when she charged it," she says, crying.

"Can you tell us what happened to our daughter?" Mr. Thompson asked.

"That's what we are trying to find out, Sir," I tell him.

"I need you to find the person who took our baby away from us, Agent," Mrs. Thompson says.

"We will find the person responsible, and your daughter will get her justice. I have a team of Agents going through everything right now. I

promise, we will find this person," I say, knowing I should never promise anything.

"Well, you made a promise, now you need to see it through, sooner rather than later," I mumble to myself.

I look at my watch and see it's a little after six o'clock. I check my app to see Michelle's currently driving home. I get up off the couch and head to the bathroom to start her bath. Tonight is about helping my wife relax, tomorrow I will focus on finding this killer.

As I shut off the water, I hear the front door open and close, letting me know Michelle is home. I walk out of the bathroom to hear her coming down the hall to the bedroom.

"Hey, love, are you ready to relax?"

"Yes, please," she says tiredly, while walking into the bathroom.

"Here let me help you," I tell her as I help her out of her clothes.

Once she's naked, I help her into the tub, and she sinks down with a sigh.

"This feels perfect, thank you so much," she sighs as I massage her shoulders.

"I know today was very hard for you, and I just want you to relax tonight."

"Being with you does relax me. You helped me today, and for that, thank you. Now how about you come join me in this hot water," she tells me with a naughty look in her eyes.

"As you wish," I tell her, grateful that she wants me to join her.

She scoots up in the tub, and I climb in behind her, pulling her back between my legs, and she lays her head on my chest.

"Remember, these little moments are what makes life so sweet," I whisper to her, before kissing the top of her head.

"Most definitely," she responds with a sigh as I feel the tension leave her body.

Three days later

My desk phone rings, and I answer, "Special Agent Chandler."

"This is Dr. Farrell," she replies, and I can't help the smile that overcomes my face hearing her voice.

I can't wait for the day when she finally takes my last name for the world to know.

"What can I do for you, Dr. Farrell," I reply.

"The DNA results are back, and the female from Lorn County is indeed Amanda Toliver," she relays.

"Thank you for the confirmation. I will call Detective Smith and let him know."

"I'll send over a copy of the results to you. Tell Detective Smith to call me when he knows which funeral home I will be coordinating with. Good luck," she adds, before hanging up.

I hang up the phone, knowing I will be tasking Detective Smith with the hard part, telling her boss/friend that she is no longer with us.

I dial the phone and wait as it rings.

"Detective Smith," he answers.

"Detective Smith, it's Agent Chandler, the DNA results are in, and they confirm the young woman is Amanda Toliver. You will need to inform Ms. Gunter and see if she will be responsible for the funeral. If so, Dr. Farrell will need to know which funeral home to contact."

"Thank you, Agent," he says, and I can hear the defeat in his voice. "I will go over and speak to her shortly. Any words of advice?"

"Just be honest and sympathetic. If you have any issues, give me a call, but I think you will be fine," I tell him before hanging up.

I walk to the conference room where the team is all gathered pouring over everything.

"The DNA results are in, and this is Amanda Toliver," I tell the room.

"So, we have Deborah Whinster from Chatam County, Krista Thompson, who was found in Pritchard County, but from Brewer County, and now Amanda Toliver from Lorn County. We are still missing the identities of the women found in Chester County and Davidson County," Kim calls out.

"Yes," I say, trying to figure out where she is going with this.

"What makes these counties so special? Why is our unsub in these areas? Are these women just victims of chance?" she asks, looking at the board.

I stare at the board as well as I ponder her question.

"Hey, Eric, I have a question," Kim whispers softly to me.

"What is it?"

"Has Detective Burton's granddaughter been found?"

"No, not that I've been told. Why?" I ask, looking at her.

"What if she's not missing?" she asks.

"I'm not following. Do you think the killer changed his MO and kidnapped her?" I ask with a furrow in my brow.

"I don't think he would change his MO, but what if she saw something that caused her to run away?" she whispers.

"You think she may have witnessed her friend's murder?"

She shrugs her shoulders. "It's possible," she says.

I look over at the pictures on the board of the young women who were killed.

"What would make her run away instead of running for help?" I ask quietly to myself.

"Exactly," Kim says beside me.

"Do me a favor, run a background check on Detective Burton, see if there is anything there that we should be concerned about."

"Yes, Sir," Kim says, leaving the conference room.

I don't want to think the Detective would have anything to do with these deaths or his granddaughter's disappearance, but I wouldn't be doing my job if I didn't at least check out his history. So far, I have only gone on his words alone.

We still need to find the identities of the other two women. I decide to call the Detectives in Chester and Davidson Counties and see if they have found anything.

As I walk into my office, my phone pings with an incoming text.

I put my phone away in my pocket, shaking my head, knowing I will be on my own for dinner. I'm happy that Kim and Michelle still have their girl time. I never want to come between best friends, and have encouraged Michelle to tell Kim about us, but I think she is afraid Kim will be upset that we didn't include her, especially for our wedding.

I've repeatedly told Michelle that Kim maybe upset, but she would never stop being there for Michelle or allow their friendship to suffer over Michelle's happiness.

As if thinking of her conjures her up, Kim knocks on my door.

"Boss, I ran the background check on the Detective, and I have to say the man is as squeaky clean as they come."

"Too squeaky?" I ask.

"He's a widow who lost his wife to cancer ten years ago, never remarried, been with the police force for thirty years, and been a detective for twenty of those thirty. His son and granddaughter are listed as his beneficiaries. The man seems to be about work and family, no hobbies, nothing. Do you think he could do all this?"

"I learned a long time ago, don't always assume someone is as good as they read on paper. He has a police background, would know how to counter forensics, it's not too far-fetched, but I don't know," I admit to her as I internally struggle with the idea of the Detective being our serial killer. "He knew one of the victims, another was found in his county, and he did want to be a part of the investigation. It's the granddaughter part that is throwing me off. He would never do anything to hurt her," I add with a deep sigh.

"We will keep looking and watching, boss," she says before adding, "I'll be leaving in a few minutes, I have dinner plans tonight."

"Okay, have a good time. I need to call the other detectives and see where they are on identifying the other two women," I respond as I pick up the phone.

I finish the calls, and both Detectives still have no identity for the females. No one in the county has reported them missing, which means they are from somewhere else. We will need to wait for the DNA results to hopefully point us in the direction of any familial matches. Someone must be missing these ladies.

Speaking of, I have not heard back from Detective Smith on how his notification went, so I decide to call him now, instead of waiting until morning, but his phone goes straight to voicemail, so I leave a message.

I pack everything up, and head home to wait for Michelle.

Chapter Seventeen

MICHELLE

I make it to the restaurant before Kim, and I get us a table. We try to have dinner, just the two of us once a month, but tonight is a special dinner. Eric never seems to mind, in fact he encourages it, and that's one of the many reasons why I love him.

I see Kim walking through the door, and I wave her over to our table.

"Hey, sorry I'm a little late," she says, "I was waiting for a background check."

"It's fine, I haven't been here long myself," I tell her, waving off her worry.

The waitress comes over, "What can I get you ladies to drink?"

"I'll have a glass of your Moscato, please," Kim says.

"Make that two, please," I chime in.

"Do you ladies need a few more minutes, or are you ready to order?"

"A few more minutes, please," Kim says.

"Sure. I'll get your drinks and be right back," she says with a smile as she walks away.

We both look over the menu, and I decide quickly on the special for the night, Lobster tails with buttered garlic potatoes.

The waitress comes back with our wine, I give her my order. Kim orders the same, and the waitress takes our menus before heading to the back.

We raise up our glasses, and I say, "Here's to twenty-four years of friendship."

"Who would have thought two girls who met during orientation would wind up as roommates and best friends," Kim says, chuckling as we both take sips of our wines.

"God, it all seems so long ago, and yet, it still feels like yesterday," I say.

"I know," she says, shaking her head.

"We're getting—"

"Don't you dare say it," I interrupt her before she says the 'O' word. "We are not there yet."

"Some days I feel like it though, like with this case," she sighs.

"I know how you feel," I admit to her. "Some days I don't know how much longer I can keep doing my job. It's so heartbreaking."

"Yeah," Kim agrees solemnly.

"So how was Heath's date?" I ask as I haven't seen anyone since the day at the park.

Kim laughs, "He says it went great, and that's all he said. He would not give the details at all."

"Oh, so he likes, likes this one," I say with a laugh. "I'm so happy for him, he deserves to find someone. We all do," I throw out there.

Kim sighs deeply before taking another sip of her wine.

"What's wrong?" I ask.

"I need your advice, I just don't know if it's smart to pull you in this," she starts.

"Whatever you tell me will always stay between us," I tell her reassuringly.

"I'm thinking about going back to DC," she says.

"Is that what you really want to do?"

"No, but I feel it's the right thing to do. If I want to keep my relationship with Declan, I'm going to need to move."

"I don't see why you can't keep the status that you currently have. Being in a secret relationship has its perks."

"Such as?"

"No one asks how the relationship is going? Nobody makes sly comments because though they think they know, they don't really know," I inform her.

"So, you and Eric are in a relationship," she says with a gasp.

"Did I say that?" I smirk before picking up my wine glass.

"How long have you two been seeing each other?" Kim asks.

"For the last year. He doesn't mind if people know, but I like how you all wonder are they, aren't they. It makes things fun and a bit dangerous. There is always the off chance that we do or say something that is going to get us caught and found out," I tell her, laughing.

"Oh my goodness, you guys are good. We have been thinking it's only been a few months," she admits.

"I need to tell you something, and I don't want you to be upset, but Eric and I got married two months ago. We went to Vegas."

"Wait, you had Elvis marry you?" she asks.

"Hell no. We found a small chapel and a priest. His brother and my sister were the only ones at the wedding, and they were there as witnesses," I admit to her.

"You got married without me?"

"Yeah, I'm sorry," I tell her sheepishly. "I knew you were going to be upset, and I've been dreading telling you," I admit.

"Oh, Shelly, I'm happy for you, I really am. It just would have been nice to have been there, but I get it. No one knew you two were in a relationship, it would have been weird to tell us you were getting married," she says, biting on the inside of her cheek.

"We do plan on telling the team, eventually. Eric wanted to do it as soon as we got back, but it was me. I just don't want the team dynamic to change just because Eric and I are married. I like our runs together with Heath, and I don't want that to change just because I'm married to your boss," I explain.

"Yeah, that would really put a damper on the fun times for sure. Don't worry, your secret is safe with me. So, being in a secret relationship is really fun?" she asks casually.

"Oh yes," I tell her, grinning.

"Maybe I'll rethink this whole move and try to enjoy the secrecy of the relationship. I'll talk to Declan and see what he thinks. Our biggest issue is Frankie," she tells me as the waitress brings our food to the table.

"Thank you," I tell her as she sets my plate in front of me. "Wow, this smells amazing," I say.

When the waitress leaves, I look at Kim and say, "Frankie isn't an issue, because you don't have those types of feelings for him. He's more like the annoying younger brother, and eventually he will find the right woman for him. Until then, you will just have to deal with his childish antics until he grows up a little more."

"This is true. I know he doesn't have real emotional feelings for me because he doesn't know me well enough. Everything he knows is superficial. I don't think we have ever really had a true heart to heart conversation," she says, pondering that thought before taking a bite of her meal.

"Does Frankie ever really have heart to heart conversations with anyone?" I ask, trying to recall all my conversations with him. I have only seen the cocky jokester.

"I don't think he has, and to be honest, I don't think he really knows how," Kim says.

"Well, here's to one day, him finding the right girl."

"Agreed," she says as we clink our glasses together.

Kim and I finish our meal, then call it a night. I feel better telling Kim the truth about Eric and I. I should have listened to him sooner. He said everything would be alright, and I can't wait to tell him he was right, well about this anyway.

Chapter Eighteen

ERIC

Michelle came home from dinner very happy last night. She finally told Kim our secret, and as I said, everything was fine.

She still doesn't want to tell the rest of the team yet, and I'm okay with her decision. I get it, she's concerned they will treat her differently. I can't say she's wrong, because I really don't know.

I know they all respect and love her, but her concerns could be valid, though I think most, if not all, already have an idea formed in their minds about us.

I doubt marriage is one of those ideas, I think to myself as I chuckle.

"What's got you so happy today, Boss?" Frankie asks. "Did you meet up with someone last night?"

"That's none of your business, Frankie," I tell him sternly, curbing my emotions.

"Sorry, Boss, didn't mean to pry," he says, taking a seat at the conference table.

"Not everyone talks about their personal life," Kim says as she comes in.

"Well hunnybun, that's because you don't have a personal life," Heath tells her.

"That you know about," Kim quips back, "I don't recall you telling us about your dates with Chris either," Kim adds.

"We have a killer to catch," Heath says, deflecting.

"Yes, we do," I tell them all. "Have we been able to identify the two Jane Does yet?"

"No, Boss. I'm hopeful that the DNA will result in helping," Heath answers.

My cell phone rings, and the caller id says it's Michelle.

"Special Agent Chandler," I answer so she knows I'm not alone.

"I have an identity on the Jane Doe found in Davidson County," she tells me.

"Who is she?"

"Her name is Sarah Anderson, and she's actually from Chatam County," Michelle informs me.

That raises the hair on the back of my neck. "Chatam County? Are you sure?"

"Yes. The familial relationship is a sister, Heather Anderson, she also lives in Chatam County. Do you want me to text you her address?"

"Yes, please, and I will call Detective Burton," I tell her.

When I hang up the phone, I look at the team and relay what Michelle just informed me.

"I found her. Her sister reported her missing ten days ago," Heath says, pulling up the missing person file in the database.

"Chatam County?" Kim asks.

I nod, then say, "I need to call Detective Burton and have him meet me at the address."

I pull my phone out, dialing the Detective's number as I walk out of the conference room.

"Eric, have you found my granddaughter?" He asks, sounding frantic.

"No, we haven't, but I do have a name on one of the Jane Does, and she's from your county," I tell him.

"I'm sorry to hear that, and I'm glad you found out who she is, but I just can't help you today. It's been almost a week since anyone has seen Rayeanne."

"I understand, I just wanted to inform you, and I'll make the notification to the next of kin," I tell him.

"If you absolutely need me to accompany you, I will, but I prefer not to leave my son if possible."

"I think I can handle this one myself," I tell him honestly, then I ask, "Would there be a reason your granddaughter would run away?"

"Run away?" he asks. "You think she may have ran away? I don't know why she would, but I'll ask my son and daughter-in-law if they know of a reason," he says.

"I'm not saying she did, but we should look at all the possibilities," I tell him.

"You're right. I'm so close to this, that I'm not thinking like a Detective right now," he admits to me.

"It's understandable. She is your only grandchild, so it would make sense that you are not leaning on your instincts right now. I just thought I would ask to see if there was a possibility, and if so, where would she go?"

"I will have to ask, because I don't have an answer to that right now," he tells me.

"If you need any help, don't hesitate to ask. We will help where we can."

"Thank you, I appreciate that. I will let you know what I find out from her parents," he tells me before hanging up.

"Kim," I call out.

"Yes, Boss," she calls back, walking toward me.

"Can you look into Rayeanne Burton's life and see if you can find a reason she could have run away, besides what we already discussed."

"Sure. I can check her internet usage, see what sites she visited, her chat histories, and I'll let you know what I find."

"Thank you. I'm heading to Chatam to inform the next of kin, let me know if there is something I need to do, while I'm there."

"When I find out something, I'll let you know," she tells me.

I walk toward the elevator, knowing my next tasks will not be an easy one.

Heather Anderson reacted to the news of her sister's death, just as I knew she would. It took me ten minutes to get her to calm down enough for me to ask her questions.

"Ms. Anderson, can you tell me why your sister would have been in Davidson County?"

"She was there for work, but when she didn't come home on the night she was supposed to, and I had not heard from her, I filed a missing per-

son's report with the local PD. They told me they would contact Davidson County, but everyday I called them, they said they had nothing for me."

"Was your sister a jogger?"

"Yes. She loves jogging, we both do. Anywhere we go, we always find a park to jog at," she informs me before asking, "Did something happen to her at the park."

"Yes, ma'am. Her body was found in the lake," I tell her.

"Oh my God, who would do this?"

"Can you think of anyone who would want to hurt your sister?"

"No, she was the kindest person who would do anything for anyone," she says, breaking down again.

She did give me the name of a funeral home that she wanted her sister to be received at, so I am currently on my way to see Michelle before I go back to the office.

Kim has not called me, so I'm not sure if that means she didn't find anything, or she hasn't unlocked everything. I'll find out more when I get to the office.

I knock on Michelle's door, causing her to look up. The smile that breaks out on her face when she sees me, causes my cock to swell, and I have to calm it down.

"Hey, how did it go?" she asks.

"About as well as expected," I say, and she nods.

Before I can say anything more, her phone rings. She holds up a finger for me to wait, then answers, putting the phone on speaker.

"State of Maine morgue, this is Dr. Farrell."

"Doctor Farrell, this is Dan from Crowley Funeral Home. I hear you will be sending me another resident," he sounds very excited, and I can't understand why.

"What resident?" she asks as I watch her body completely tense up.

"Sarah Anderson? I just got off the phone with her sister, Heather," Dan says.

She looks up at me, and I nod.

"Oh, I hadn't been informed yet, but yes, I will prepare the body for transport, will you be able to receive her tomorrow?"

"Of course. Will you be transporting her yourself? I would really like to meet you and discuss your last lecture on forensic anatomy," he tells her.

"I'm not sure what my day will be like tomorrow, but if I can, I will," she tells him politely.

"Great, then hopefully I will see you tomorrow. Have a great evening, Doctor Farrell," he tells her before hanging up.

"What was that about?" I ask her.

"What?"

"You tensed up the minute you heard his voice?"

She sighs, "I didn't realize I did that. I don't know, there is something off about him. The Whinster's used his funeral home for their daughter. When I called to confirm transport, he was for the lack of a better word, fangirling. I can handle fans, and am used to it, especially since he told me he has been to every one of my conferences, but something about the way he did it was a little off putting. His tune changed when he heard who the victim was, apparently he knows the family."

"How well?"

"Their families attend the same church, so I will assume really well, since he told me he needed to call them right away," she says, looking up at me.

"Do you have his full name?" I ask her.

"Yeah," she says, writing it down and passing it to me.

"I will do a check on him. It may be nothing, but the fact that he has been to all of your seminars and wants to speak to you about forensics, sets off some alarm bells inside of me," I admit to her.

She nods. "I understand."

"I'll let you get back to work, since he," pointing toward the phone, "told you what I came here to tell you. I'll see you at home tonight."

"See you tonight," she tells me with a smile, and I leave.

I need to get back to the office and run a check on this Dan Leary. Anyone who makes my wife tense up, is definitely someone to look into. Especially if he has been attending all her conferences and trying to get close to her.

Chapter Nineteen

ERIC

When I walk in the office, I hand Kim the piece of paper with Dan's name. "Can you run this name for me?"

"Sure, Boss," she says, going back to her computer.

I walk in the conference room and see the rest of the team looking through the files we currently have on these cases.

"Do we have anything yet?" I ask, frustration boiling inside of me, knowing we could have another victim any day now.

"Boss, unfortunately we have nothing. No forensics, no evidence, and no real suspects," Declan tells me.

Kim walks in, "Well, I may have something," she says. "You asked me to run a background check on Dan Leary, and guess who he has familial ties to?"

"Who?" I ask.

"Detective Burton. Seems Dan is the brother to Detective Burton's daughter-in-law, and not only that, but he is a registered sex offender."

"Excuse me?" Heath says.

"He has a sealed juvenile record, but I was able to get it opened, and it seems when Mr. Leary was seventeen, he was caught in a park and charged with public lewdness, indecent exposure, as well as publication intoxication."

"I think we need to have a conversation with Mr. Leary," I say. "Especially since his niece is missing, and he didn't sound like a devastated man on the phone," I add as I walk to the elevators with the team closely on my heels.

"You talked to him already?" Heath asks.

"No, when I went by Mi—Dr. Farrell's office to inform her the name of the funeral home that Ms. Anderson stated she wanted her sister's remains sent to, he happened to call, and she had him on speaker phone. He's very infatuated with Dr. Farrell and her seminars, especially the forensics," I inform them as we make our way to the vehicle.

"That's not scary at all," Kim mutters sarcastically.

We drive to Chatam County, pulling up outside the funeral home. Someone is locking the front door of the building.

"That's Dan Leary," Kim says, looking at the picture she downloaded from his files.

I get out of the vehicle, and he turns to look at me.

"I'm sorry, but we are closed for the night. If you leave me your name and number, I will get back with you in the morning to make arrangements for your loved one," he says.

"I'm not here for your services, Mr. Leary. I have some questions for you. My name is Special Agent Chandler of the Behavioral Unit."

"Behavioral Unit, as in the FBI?" he asks.

"The one," I tell him.

"Oh wow, how can I help you?" he says, almost gushing.

"Mr. Leary, I'm surprised you are so enthusiastic, given that your niece has been missing for almost a week," I tell him.

"What are you talking about? My sister hasn't told me my niece is missing?" he says, completely shocked by the news.

"When was the last time you saw her?"

"I've never met her in person," he admits as his shoulders slump down. "I've only seen pictures of her over the years."

"Why is that?" I ask.

"Because I was stupid when I was seventeen. My girlfriend had broken up with me, and I got drunk. Somehow, I ended up in the park down from our house. I was drunk, distraught, and didn't realize what I was doing. I didn't even know there was a kid in the park. Anyways, someone called the cops, and now I'm registered as a sex offender for a stupid thing I did as a kid."

"And because of that, you are not allowed around kids," I add.

"Correct. That's why I run the family business. When there is a service here with family and friends for the viewing, I have to leave it all to one of my assistants to handle while I sit at home by myself. It's all unfair really, I would never hurt any child. It was just a stupid mistake," he whispers the last part. "I need to call my sister," he quickly adds, patting his pockets for his phone.

"Before you do that, is it true you knew Deborah Whinster?"

"Yes, we attend the same church. I went to school with her parents. It's awful what happened to her," he says.

"How are you able to go to church, being a registered sex offender?" I ask.

"I'm always the last one in, I stand at the back of the church, and when the service is over, I'm the first one to leave, not to mention there are plenty of police officers that also attend the service, and keep an eye on me."

I nod my head.

"Agent, I really am not a bad person. I made one mistake, and it's cost me a lot in my life, to include spending time with my family and getting to know my niece," he says, looking completely devastated.

"Thank you, Mr. Leary for speaking with me. I'll let you call your sister," I say, heading back to the vehicle. "Oh, one more question, do you do any jogging?"

"Every other night, I go to the park to run when everyone else has gone home."

"Ever go to other counties?"

"Sometimes, if I want to get away for a little while, I may go camping or explore around. Why?" he asks.

"Just wondering," I say, making a note of that as I get back in the vehicle.

The windows roll up, and Heath asks, "What did you think of that, Boss?"

"I don't know. Part of me thinks he isn't our unsub. He was truly devastated to learn his niece was missing and his sister had not called him, but he has means and opportunity. I'm not ready to rule him out," I say, with a sigh.

"Rayeanne wouldn't know him, if she's never been allowed to meet him," Kim says.

"True. Were you able to get into any of her social accounts?" I ask. Kim.

"Yes, and there is absolutely nothing there. No signs of her chatting with anyone other than the girls from the soccer team and school. No mentions of any boys, everything was about school work and college, so if there was anything, it had to have been done or said in person," Kim says, sounding frustrated.

"We should question the girls on the traveling soccer team, maybe they can also help us with Krista Thompson, not just Rayeanne," I tell the team.

"I'll ask Krista's parents for the roster," Kim says.

We get back to the office, and it's time to call it a night.

There is something in the back of my mind that is nagging at me, but I can't grasp what it could be. I get in my car and head home to Michelle for the night, knowing it's been a long day and a lot of information. Maybe after a good night's sleep, it will come to me.

Chapter Twenty

Unknown

"Why are we here again?" I whisper, while standing in the trees looking over the big building and the parking lot.

She intrigues me, the demon whispers in my head.

The woman in question comes out of the building, walking to her car. Since we first saw her, he has been infatuated with her. Following her everywhere, from work to the park on nights when she runs, even to dinner with her friend.

"You know she is never alone, and you've seen the man," I whisper to him, like anyone could hear us standing in the woods.

So what, he won't be able to save her when it's her time, none of them will be able to save her. We just have to plan our attack precisely. She was meant for us, you saw the look in her green eyes. So sweet and caring, we can break her, and she will be our victory, he tells me as we watch her get in her car.

"I don't want to break her," I whimper back.

It's not your choice to make, it's mine. She will be our next, he says as we watch her drive away.

He's rubbing my penis, and I can see his thoughts. They are dirty and vile, the things he wants to do to her. He's most excited to show her how the others died, choking on his cock as he shoved it so far down their throats until they stopped breathing, while he pinched their nipples hard.

He has kept them all in a zip lock bag, stored in a secret pocket in our jacket. Sometimes I catch him taking them out and touching them, as he remembers what they felt like on each girl.

"Stop it," I berate him for his thoughts.

One day, you will join in and enjoy everything we do, he says, laughing, before turning around and walking back deep into the woods.

"Never," I say, but he keeps laughing.

Chapter Twenty-One

MICHELLE

"Eric, I'm tired," I tell him, breathlessly. We have been sparring for the last hour and a half, and I can't do it anymore.

"I'm sorry, hun, my mind is all over the place, and I was trying to work through everything about these cases," he tells me.

"I get it, and I understand, but I need to tap out."

We have sparring sessions in the gym of our apartment complex twice a week as a date night, but tonight, I can tell Eric is trying to work out his frustrations. I did my best to keep up, but I'm completely spent and in need of a shower.

I grab my gear and walk back to the apartment. Eric catches up as I get to the door.

"I'm sorry, Shell," he tells me.

"No need to apologize. How about I make us dinner tonight after we shower, and you try to relax."

He smirks at me, "So we are having grilled cheese sandwiches and tomato soup?"

"Yep," I say, as I pop the p. He knows I'm not much of a cook, but he allows me these little things.

We both jump in the shower, and I take my time washing his body, as I feel the tension leave him to only be replaced with a hungry desire.

I drop down to my knees and wrap my mouth around his erect cock, while circling my tongue around his head.

"Oh God, Shell, you feel so good," he whispers.

I suck him in deeper, allowing him to hit the back of my throat, causing me to gag a little.

I relax my throat and take him a little deeper, as I moan, sending vibrations through his cock.

I hear him suck in a breath and gasp.

"Yeah, just like that, baby," he tells me, placing his hands on my head, and wrapping my hair around one fist.

"God, you are so beautiful like this," he tells me, and I can't help the blush that creeps up my face.

I love when he talks to me like this, especially when he loses control when I do this. I take his cock all the way back into my throat as far as I can, gagging and moaning at the same time.

"Oh fuck," he says, shoving my head down on his cock more chasing his release.

I feel his cock swelling, so I reach up and massage his balls, causing him to breathe in sharply.

Before I know it, he's spilling his cum down my throat. I lick him clean, before releasing his softened cock.

He helps me stand up, then kisses me breathless.

"Thank you, baby," he says when he breaks the kiss

"You are very welcome, now let's clean up so I can make us a gourmet dinner," I tell him as we both laugh.

When we get out of the shower, I quickly throw on a pair of leggings, t-shirt, and head to the kitchen to start on our dinner.

Eric comes out, looking more relaxed than before, and I can't help the smile that crosses my face. *Yeah, I did that*, I think to myself as I hum some tune I don't even know.

I take our dinner to the table, and we eat.

After dinner, Eric's phone rings, and he looks at the caller id.

"Detective Burton, is everything okay?" I hear him ask.

"Yes, I did have a conversation with him."

"No, I can't," I hear him sigh.

"Still no word on your granddaughter, then?" He asks.

"Yes, I will talk with you tomorrow. Good night," he tells him as he hangs up.

"They still haven't found her?"

He shakes his head.

"Any reason why she would run away?" I ask.

"Not any that her family knows about," he tells me.

I wrap my arms around him, laying my head on his chest. "I'm sorry," I tell him.

He wraps his arms around me, and we stand like that for a few minutes before I grab his hand and pull him to bed.

While we are lying in bed, I make the decision. "I think it's time. I'm ready to tell the team about our marriage. I'd like to do it over dinner, if you are okay with that," I say softly.

"I'm more than okay and ready to tell them. You guys are running tomorrow, right?"

"Yeah, it's a run day, do you think I should wait a day?"

"No, I think tomorrow will be fine. We can give everyone an opportunity to go home and clean up before meeting us."

"Sounds good. I'll put it in the group chat tomorrow, when Kim sends it out," I tell him, before kissing his lips goodnight, then cuddle up next to him and fall asleep with his arm wrapped around me.

The next day, my phone pings with an incoming message.

Kim: Run at 5pm?

I respond quickly.

Me: I'll be there.

Heath: Absolutely

Declan: I'll pass today.

Frankie: I'm in.

Me: Can we all meet for dinner tonight after the run? There is something I would like to discuss with everyone.

Heath: Can we shower first?

Looks like the majority of the gang is all in. I notice Eric didn't respond, and it's likely because he is talking with Detective Burton today.

I prep Sarah Anderson for transport to the funeral home and ask one of the guys to take her. Dan seems nice enough on the phone, but I have no desire to meet him in person. He seems too eager to meet me, and those vibes just rub me the wrong way.

I continue doing paperwork and checking for DNA results on our last victim that has yet to be identified, but still no matches in the system.

At four forty-five, I change into my running gear, locking up the office, and heading to the park. When I pull into the parking lot, Kim and Heath are already there.

"What's the big news, hunny," he asks.

"You will find out with everyone else, just calm down," I tell him.

"That's not fair. Kimmy and I should know before anyone else, we are your bitches," he says, but I'm saved when Frankie pulls in.

"Soon," I say, as we all stretch and head out on our run.

Chapter Twenty-Two

Eric

I'm at the apartment, getting dressed for dinner, waiting for Michelle to come home. I'm so glad she is ready to tell everyone. I don't know what changed her mind, but I'm ecstatic for this dinner.

I think back to my conversation with Detective Burton this morning as I button up my shirt.

"Of course, I checked out your family, Detective Burton. I wouldn't be a good Agent if I didn't. Two of the victims are from your county, one of

the victims played on a soccer team with your granddaughter in a county where the tournament was taking place, and your granddaughter is missing. I would be remiss not to cover all the bases," I tell him, standing in my office.

"I understand that, Agent, but Dan has never been around Rayeanne. Even though he was only a drunk kid, we have ensured that he has never violated any of the restrictions that were bestowed on him by the law."

"That's what he told me, but he also informed me he is a jogger and he visits other counties to get away from Chatam County. He's also attended several of Dr. Farrell's conferences and had an understanding of forensics. Put yourself in my shoes Detective, if you were working this case, would you not consider him a prime suspect if you didn't know him. Especially with the record and being flagged as a sexual predator."

"I didn't know he was attending conferences," he says, sounding very shocked by the news. After a few minutes of silence while he ponders what I told him, he states, "You are right, and I understand what you are saying, but this is also a lot of stress on my daughter-in-law. First, her daughter is missing. We don't know if she has been taken or if she simply ran away and from what? We don't know. Now, her brother is a suspect, not only in potential murders but her daughter's disappearance. It's a lot to deal with all at once," he says.

"I know, but I also know you are very close to these cases, so I'm going to have to ask you to sit out on this." I raise my hand to stop him from speaking. "I'm not saying to stop looking for your granddaughter, but to step back from the homicide cases. You should be out there looking for your granddaughter," I tell him.

"Thank you," he whispers as his shoulders sag.

"When was the last time you slept, or even eaten anything?" I ask him.

"I don't know, honestly. I'm on the streets every night, looking for her everywhere," he admits.

"You are not going to be any good to her if you are not taking care of yourself. You need to go home, eat a sandwich, and get a couple of hours of sleep. Maybe when you wake up, something will occur to you to check next," I tell him.

"You are right. I keep telling my daughter-in-law and son the same things, but I'm not good about taking my own advice, obviously," he says, rubbing his hands down his unshaven face.

"Then maybe it's time you start. A couple of hours won't hurt you, it may even help."

"Okay, thank you, Agent Chandler, and please let me know if you find out anything more."

"I will. I promise," I tell him, walking him to the elevator.

I walked back to my office and checked my cell to see the group chat and Michelle inviting everyone to dinner for an announcement, our announcement. I can't help the smile that spreads across my face knowing after tonight, we will no longer need to keep a secret.

I hear the front door open, pulling me out of my thoughts.

"Hey babe," I call out.

"Hi, handsome. Give me ten minutes to shower," she says, heading straight for the bathroom.

I hear the shower turn on, and I know she will stick to those ten minutes. I finish putting on my shoes, when the shower turns off. I smile, she is so predictable.

When she comes out, she goes straight for the closet, and comes out with a pair of jeans and light-weight blue shirt.

It doesn't take her long to get her clothes on.

"Calm down, it will take Heath at least an hour before he is ready," I tell her.

"I want to get there before anyone. I'm going to need a drink in me, I'm so nervous," she says, rushing into the bathroom to comb out her hair.

"Shell, it's not like you need to impress anyone, they already love you, and I know they will be happy for us."

"I know," she says, laying down her comb. "I just worry this will change the dynamics for all of us, and I don't want that."

"Nothing needs to change, and you can reiterate that tonight after we tell them," I tell her, grabbing her by the hips. "Everything will be fine, I promise," I say, kissing her lips.

She melts into me as she always does.

"You're right, I need to not overthink everything."

She walks away to put her shoes on, then says with a deep breath, "Okay, I'm ready."

I smile, taking her hand and leading her out of the apartment.

We are the first to arrive at the restaurant, just as she wanted it, we wait at the bar, and I order her a wine to help calm her nerves.

Twenty minutes later, Kim and Declan walk in, and I see the smile spread across Michelle's face. I look back at Kim and Declan and wonder if I'm missing something. Heath walks in, with a guy I don't know.

"Hey Boss, this is Chris, Chris, this is my Boss, Special Agent Eric Chandler," Heath says as he introduces me to the gentleman.

"Please call me Eric, it's nice to meet you Chris," I say, shaking his hand.

"Chris, it's so nice to see you again," Michelle says.

"And you as well. I hope you don't mind me tagging along?" he asks.

"Of course not," she tells him with a smile.

Kim's phone rings, and she looks down at it, shaking her head, and ignoring it. The door opens, and Frankie walks in, at first glance he looks upset, but then I see a smile break out on his face when he sees us all there.

"Hey everyone, sorry I'm late. Chris, right?" He says to Heath's friend.

"Yes, and your, Frankie?"

"Yes, nice to see you again."

"You as well," Chris responds, standing close to Heath.

I flag the waitress down letting her know we are ready for a table now.

She sits us immediately at a long table in the back, handing out menus and taking drink orders.

We all order our meals, and she leaves us.

"So, what's the big news you want to share, Shelly?" Heath asks, looking intrigued.

She quickly takes a sip of her wine, looks up at me, then at the rest of the team and then blurts out, "Eric and I are married."

"What? When? How long?" Questions getting thrown at us all at once from everyone but Kim.

"Calm down," I say. "Michelle and I have been dating for over a year, and two months ago, we got married."

"Wow," Frankie says.

"And you didn't invite us to the wedding," Heath says, pouting.

"We didn't get married here, we went to Vegas," Michelle says.

Heath gasps, "Elvis married you?"

"Hell no," Shell says, "We found a cute chapel and a priest to marry us."

"Wait," Heath raises his hand, looking at Kim. "How come you don't look shocked?" He asks her. "Did you know about this?" He gasps, "Did you go to the wedding?"

"No." she responds, but Heath is staring daggers at her. "Seriously, I only found out a couple of days ago," Kim tells the table. "I was just as shocked as you are right now," she tells Heath.

"So, you knew before me?" Heath pouts.

"That's best friend privilege," she tells him and he gasps.

"I thought we were all besties."

"We are," Michelle quickly jumps in to say, "But I have known Kim a lot longer and thought she needed to know first. I'm sorry, but I promise guys, we will hold another ceremony and a reception, here, for all of you," she tells the team. "I didn't want anyone to know for a while, because I didn't want the dynamics in the team to change," she admits.

"That is never going to happen, but now I know who put the marks on you for sure. We all assumed you two were in a relationship, but we weren't quite sure," Heath admits.

"We know," Michelle says, laughing. "It was fun watching you all question are they, aren't they, and it made our relationship more exciting," she tells them.

"Congratulations to you both," Declan says.

"Yes, congratulations," everyone at the table says, raising their drinks.

"Thank you all," Michelle and I say at the same time.

We enjoy our dinner and conversation for the rest of the evening, and I can tell Michelle is more relaxed now that the truth is out. She looks over at me with a huge smile, and I lean down kissing her on the lips.

"No more hiding," I whisper to her.

"No more hiding," she agrees.

Chapter Twenty-Three

MICHELLE

After our wonderful dinner, Eric and I went home and talked about having another wedding for the team so Kim can be my maid-of-honor. I know it still upsets Kim that she wasn't at our wedding the first time.

"I know I already told the team we would have one, without discussing it with you first, but I really think the team wants this," I tell him.

"I'd be on board for marrying you again, Mrs. Chandler," he tells me, pulling me into his arms. "I would also be on board with having a summer wedding at our new cabin, so we could have it outside by the lake," he adds.

This man never ceases to amaze me. "I love that idea," I smile up at him.

"Good, then let's plan a summer wedding," he says.

"Okay, sounds like a plan."

I know Kim will be excited to help me plan a wedding, and I will be happy to have her help.

The next morning, I get to work feeling so much better now that everyone is aware of our marriage. Well, his team knows, I guess it's time to tell Janine.

"Good morning, Dr. Farrell," Janine says.

"It's actually Dr. Chandler," I tell her. "I will be submitting the official documentation for the name change," I add.

"Congratulations, Doctor," she says with a laugh.

"Did you know?" I ask.

"That you got married, no, but I did know pretty quickly you two were an item."

"Huh," I say.

"When was the wedding?"

"Two months ago in Vegas," I tell her.

"Oh wow. Was his team there?"

"No, it was just us. My sister and his brother came as our witnesses. We just told his team about us last night at dinner," I tell her as a sigh leaves me. "We are planning to have another wedding this summer, and everyone will be invited this time," I add letting her know she will be too.

"Sounds like fun," she says with a smile.

I continue walking to my office to boot up the computer and check my emails. I want to send Kim a text to start the wedding planning. We only have three months, since I want a July wedding. I can't help the giddiness that takes over me.

Three days later

Kim and I spent the weekend discussing wedding plans, and I even took her out to the cabin Eric bought us so she could see it for herself. We have a preliminary plan for set up and decorations. I took her down by the lake, showing her a spot in the backyard that would be perfect for the set-up.

"Oh, Shelly, this is beautiful," Kim says.

"It really is," I say, taking in the breathtaking view of the lake. "What do you think of an arch, placed right here in front of the lake, with a eucalyptus garland wrapped around it, and purple orchids placed in the garland?"

"Sounds beautiful, and we can set the chairs up back here, with white peonies attached at the end of each aisle, and a red carpet coming down the middle," she says dreamily.

"It will be stunning," I say with a smile as I imagine it.

"What do you plan to wear?" Kim asks.

"I plan to wear the same dress I wore in Vegas, a white, pencil silhouette, knee-length, sleeveless, with a ruching v-neck, chiffon dress with a ruching bow, and split back. It's simple, yet elegant at the same time."

"Perfect. We just need to decide on the bouquets, and what color you want my maid-of honor dress," she tells me.

"What color do you want to wear?" I ask.

"How about a beautiful olive green," she tells me with a smile.

"You already have the dress picked out, don't you?" I ask with a laugh.

"I do, and it's so pretty," she says, gushing.

"Then you should absolutely wear it."

I turn back and look at the lake with a sigh. "It's going to be a beautiful wedding," I say.

We discussed whether to cater a meal or do finger foods. That decision is still up in the air at this time, but I feel like we have enough to start diving into the planning, and though it will be a small wedding, I still want it to be perfect.

Now it's Monday, and the mornings are always busy, between paperwork and going over any lab results that may have come in, but after this weekend, my mind just isn't on work.

I shouldn't be this obsessed with a wedding, I mean, I am already married to Eric, however I keep finding my thoughts straying to ideas for the wedding, and jotting down notes to discuss with Kim later.

I sigh and sit back in my chair, knowing I should be more invested in helping the victims, especially the Jane Doe that is still currently in my morgue unidentified from Chester County, but my mind just isn't today.

My phone pings with an incoming text.

Kim: Run today?

Me: Yes, please. I think I need it to focus my mind.

Heath: I'm in.

> **Declan: Can't today.**
>
> **Frankie: I'm out.**
>
> **Me: Okay, see you two at the normal time.**

I place my phone on the desk, hoping to be able to focus on something more than wedding plans now that I know we will be running this evening. A run always helps me, so hopefully it will today.

I busy myself with menial tasks for an upcoming conference that I will be speaking at in a couple of weeks. I'm not sure if that funeral director, Dan will show up, but with the amount of suspicion on him, I really hope not. Something about him just doesn't feel right when I hear his voice.

I shake off my thoughts about Dan and continue putting my lecture together. Before I realize it, the day is gone, and it's four forty-five. Time for me to change into my workout clothes and head to the park.

Chapter Twenty-Four

MICHELLE

When I pull into the parking lot of the park, it's pretty empty for a Monday evening. There are only two vehicles in the parking lot, which is surprising since the sun is shining and the temperature is seventy-eight degrees. With daylight savings time, the sun stays out a little longer now.

Seeing that I'm the first one to arrive, I get out of the car and begin my stretching while I wait. I get a niggling feeling in the back of my neck, that I'm being watched. I look around the parking lot and toward the running path, I don't see anyone, but I feel like someone is close by. I opt to go back and sit in my car while I wait for Kim and Heath to get here.

Just before I reach my driver's door, I hear a voice that sends chills down my spine. "Hello, Doctor, I've been waiting for you," the voice behind me says, and just as I'm turning around, I feel the punch to the side of my head, and I begin to lose my balance as I drop my phone, then another punch hits me, knocking me on the ground and right before I blackout, I feel arms lift me up.

I come to, feeling hands and air on my breasts and a body on top of me. My sports bra is no longer on, and I can feel the wetness of leaves, dirt, and something hard—maybe sticks—digging into my back. I realize quickly I am no longer in the parking lot, but maybe a wooded area by the amount of dirt I can feel underneath me.

How long was I out for?

"I've been waiting for you since I saw you at the lake," he says, jarring me back to my current situation.

The voice sounds somewhat familiar, but I can't quite place it, as I continue to keep my eyes closed and listen to what is going on.

I don't hear anything outside of this man's whispers and heavy breathing. I can feel his soft hands on me as he continues to fondle my breasts, while making lewd comments. "Oh, these are more perfect than I imagined they were," he says, placing his mouth around my nipple and sucking hard. He's moaning, and I can feel the hardness of his penis as he pushes into my leg.

My body automatically tenses up, and I feel like a million bugs are crawling all over my skin as he continues touching me. His touch is rough and painful, and I'm trying very hard to keep my breathing even, but feeling his body on top of mine, and his mouth on my nipple as his tongue flicks the hardened bud, my body doesn't pretend to not be disgusted. I'm immediately immobilized by fear and panic. I know what he plans to do, and I can hear my racing heartbeat in my own ears. I try to calm the panic enough to think. *Think Michelle, you must do something, you can't let him do this to you*, I inwardly tell myself. My stomach continues to revolt from his touches, and I'm afraid I may get sick right here. I need to find a way out of this, for myself and for Eric.

"Absolutely perfect," he says as he goes back to fondling. "I'm sorry we can't have the beautiful scenery as the others did, by the lake, but I knew it was only a matter of time before your friends showed up, and I needed to improvise. Still, the woods are very lovely, and I'm going to enjoy taking your body," he says, laughing maniacally before grabbing the hem of my leggings to pull them down.

I open my eyes, the sun is so bright that I'm unable to keep them open, I immediately close them again. When I reopen them, I'm able to see the sun directly above, peeking through the trees. I look at the man who currently has his hands at the hem of my leggings, and I'm momentarily stunned for just a second before my survival instincts kick in, and I remember everything Eric has taught me.

I quickly swing into action, immediately using the palm of my hand and strike in an upward and forward motion against his nose, hearing a crunch. I know it's broken, and I don't care. His blood is pouring down on me as he screams, grabbing his nose. I use my foot to kick him in the groin before pushing him away from me with my foot and rolling to the other side away from him.

I get up on my knees and with my hands, push to my feet. I quickly take in my surroundings, and I am indeed in the woods, but which woods? I look around, but we are so far in, I can't tell how far away from a road or residential area we are.

My heart is beating fast as I hear him start to get to his feet. "Thank you, Eric, for teaching me self-defense," I whisper to myself as fear and adrenaline kick in, and I begin running.

I look back to see where he is. That was a mistake, the man is on his feet, and he is coming after me.

I hear him call out from behind me, "You bitch, I am going to enjoy killing you more than I did the others. You can't get away."

"The hell I can't," I mutter to myself as I continue running. I have no idea where I am at, so I'm not sure what direction I am running in, but I continue running as if my life depends on it, because it really does.

I put as much speed in my run as I can, but the terrain is unstable with all the trees and roots sticking up from the ground. The leaves are slippery from last night's rain, and several times I have had to catch myself, otherwise I would have fallen.

"You can't run from me," he calls out, and I know he's not far behind me.

"Shit," I breathe out. "Where do I go?" I mutter to myself. *Have they realized I've been taken? Are they looking for me? Of course, they do and are, just keep running,* I tell myself internally.

"I can hear you breathing my little slut. Don't worry, I'll have you breathing and screaming really hard before the night is through," he taunts me, sounding closer than before.

I don't dare look back, I keep pushing, my adrenaline is the only thing keeping me going right now.

"Got you," he says as his hands grab me.

I let out a scream as he pushes me to the ground face first, and he is on top of my back.

Chapter Twenty-Five

ERIC

M y phone rings, and it's Kim calling.

"What's going on Kim?" I ask, knowing she is supposed to be running with Michelle.

"Eric, have you heard from Shelly?" she asks, sounding panicked and breathing hard.

The hairs on my neck stand up with that one question, "No, not since I saw your group text about the run. What's going on, Kim?" I ask frantically but try to stay calm.

"Heath and I got to the park, Shelly's car is here, but she is not. I thought she may have started without us, since we were a little late getting here, so I left Heath at the beginning of the path, and I ran ahead hoping to catch up with her, but when I got back to Heath, he said she never came around."

"Did you call her phone?" I ask, immediately picking up the desk phone and dialing her number. I ignore the way my hands are shaking, right now, I need to focus on the task at hand.

"Yeah, while I was running and no answer," Kim says as I hear the ring in my ear.

"Wait, what is that noise?" I hear Kim ask.

Then I hear the ringing of the phone. "Kim, what is going on?"

"Eric, we found her phone, it was underneath her car. Something's happened to her, I can feel it." Kim says, panic and fear lacing her voice.

"I'm on my way, call the others so we can start a search." I tell her, running out of the office and to the elevators. I hit the button and quickly realize taking the stairs will be faster than waiting for the elevator.

I run down the stairs, fear spreading throughout my body for my wife. Once I'm on the ground floor, I race to the parking lot, and get to the park in five minutes, breaking every speeding law known to man. The team minus Kim, is in the parking lot waiting for me when I pull up.

I quickly jump out of the vehicle, "Where is Kim?" I ask, not caring that there is panic in my voice. My wife is missing, and I don't have time to be a boss if she is being hurt.

"Right here," she says, running up out of breath. "I went and checked by the lake since the serial killer likes to take his victims there, but she was nowhere around the area."

"We don't know that it's the serial rapist/killer who has her," I seethe, pissed that she wasted precious time looking at a lake.

"She fits his profile, blond, green eyes, and she likes to run," Kim practically screams at me, and I know it's fear for her best friend.

"It could be that creep Dan from Chatam County," I throw out with every ounce of frustration I have in me.

"And he could be our serial killer," she counters back, just as frustrated.

"If you're right and he is the serial killer, obviously he's been watching her, and if that's true, then he would know all of you would be coming, so he would have to take her somewhere close, but not too close," I say looking around, taking in my surroundings as I try to calm my frantic beating heart enough to think logically.

I see thick woods across from the parking lot and road. The trees aren't thick with leaves yet, so with as bright as the sun is shining, we should be able to see through them.

"We need to fan out and check the woods, it's the only other place he could have taken her quickly, without being seen, that would also give him privacy," I say.

We run over to the woods, fear coursing through me that I'm too late to save my wife. As soon as we get into the woods, I see I was right, there is enough light from the sun to see in the woods. I begin calling Michelle's name. Hopefully if she was able to get away, she will know to run towards my voice.

"MICHELLE," I call out.

"SHELLY," I hear Heath and Kim call out, while we all fan out and search for her.

I come upon a spot deep in the area riddled with wet leaves and sticks. It looks like the wet dirt from the rain has been disturbed. I look down by the tree and find her sports bra, there is also blood on the ground.

Panic begins to set in, so paralyzing, I'm frozen with fear. My worst nightmare flashes in my mind as I take in the blood.

Frankie comes up next to me, "Is that...?" he asks.

I won't let him finish that question. I can't allow the fear and panic to take over. I need to find my wife, and I need to find her quickly. So I quickly say, "I don't know if it's her blood or his, but yes, that is her sports bra."

I look around the ground for tracks to tell me if she ran off and which direction. Since the ground is still wet, I can make out two sets of footprints. One looks to be a female, and the other a heavy-footed male.

"This way," I say, heading in the direction of the footprints and blood spots that I see on the ground.

A few minutes later, I hear a woman's scream. I know immediately that scream is coming from Michelle, and I sprint toward the sounds, with Frankie on my heels.

"You bitch, look at what you did to my face," I hear a man say, then I hear a slap.

As I get closer to the sound of the voice I heard, I notice the area is a clearing, and I see Michelle on the ground fighting, and it's, no, it can't be.

What the hell? I stand here shocked by who it is, then I realize Father Mullen is on top of her, trying to pin her down.

"Leave her alone," I hear Father Mullen say.

"NO," a deeper, more gravelly voice says, "She's a fighter and will make us feel so good."

"This is God's way of telling you to stop," Father Mullen says.

A low chuckle fills the air. "There's no stopping me, you know that," the deeper voice says, and it seems that deep voice is also coming from Father Mullen as well.

"What the hell?" Frankie whispers, echoing my thoughts as I try to grasp the situation in front of me.

Michelle grunts, and my instincts kick in at hearing her struggle. I run forward, tackling the asshole like I'm a linebacker from a professional football team or something. I tackle him off my wife and hear heavy footsteps from my team entering the clearing, letting me know they are here. I know that they'll help Michelle while I deal with this asshole.

I hear the father whimpering beneath me, glancing down, I notice his eyes are glassy and filled with pain. It's when I'm looking into his eyes, that he whispers, "Thank you."

I have no idea what is going on, all I do know is that he needs professional help, but it doesn't negate the fact that he's killed countless women. I glance over at Michelle, my heart racing, but seeing Kim and Heath holding on to her, helping her to feet, and Heath giving his shirt to cover her, has my worry easing. She's alive, although there is a red mark on her face from where the fucker slapped her, and I can also see the dirt from the ground caked on her as well.

As if she can feel me, she looks over seeing that I am assessing her, and she nods her head, letting me know she is otherwise okay, and I take a deep breath feeling the relief course through me that she is alive.

Frankie comes up beside me, and together, he and I lift Father Mullen up off the ground, escorting him to the car. He has a lot of questions to answer.

Once Father Mullen is in the backseat, I search out Michelle. I watch as Kim opens her passenger door for Michelle. Michelle looks up at me and nods her head in understanding, knowing I need to take the priest to Headquarters, but also knowing I want her with me.

Sometimes making tough decisions makes us feel like we are making the wrong ones. I feel like I'm having to choose my job over my wife right now, and the pressure in my chest is weighing heavy on me.

When we get back to the building, I allow Frankie and Heath to take the priest upstairs and place him in an interrogation room that's down the hall from our office area.

Kim pulls into the parking lot with Michelle. I rush to the passenger door, needing to hold my wife. I see she is still wearing Heath's shirt, and I help her out of the car, noticing she has blood on her hands. I pull her into my arms and ask, "Are you okay?"

"I'll have a headache for a little while, and my face may sport a bruise or two, but physically, I'm okay. Mentally, it might take me a little while," she admits.

I look at Kim, "I need you to interrogate him since you have a background in psychology. There is something off with him."

"There is. I think he possibly suffers from some form of Schizophrenia or even multiple personalities. He was doing a lot of arguing with himself," Michelle says, then asks, "Can I listen in while you interview him?"

"Behind the glass?" Kim asks, and Michelle nods.

"Yeah, I'll be there as well," I say, holding Michelle close to me.

We take the elevator to our floor, and I show Michelle to the bathroom, giving her the opportunity to clean up a bit. When she comes out instead of leading her into the office, Michelle and I go into the room next door to interrogation to listen in on the interview. Frankie is already in there setting up the recording.

We watch as Kim walks into the room.

"Where's the pretty blond Doctor?" Father Mullen asks, but it sounds like the one who was on top of Michelle, not the one who was thanking me.

"You like blonds, huh?" she asks.

"Yes, their hair glows like a halo when the sun and water reflects off them. Especially when I take them from behind. Mmmm, they feel so good," he says, closing his eyes, like he's picturing them.

"Why?" Kim asks simply.

He opens his eyes back up and looks at her, "That's what they all ask," he says with a smirk. "The minute they open their eyes, and I'm pumping inside them, they all ask why. It's their fault really, they taught us to be this way," he says, not making sense.

"Who?" Kim asks.

His demeanor changes and then Father Mullen says softly, "Don't listen to the demon, he's bad. He doesn't listen, and he won't get out of my head. I have prayed so hard that God will take him out of me, but he doesn't."

"What happened?" Kim asks.

"I was born an orphan, raised in a catholic orphanage. When I was six, the nuns would call me into their rectory. At first, they would undress in front of me, make me touch and squeeze their breasts. Then I would get whooped for being a naughty boy. Not long after that I was being told to touch one of them everywhere, and the other would hit me. They would hit me if I didn't touch, and they would hit me for touching. It became too much for me to handle and comprehend," he said softly.

Then the one he calls the demon came back, "Oh, our boy here couldn't handle the whoopings, even now thinking about them years later, his mind is so soft, but when I took over those sisters taught me so much."

"How old was he then?"

"Twelve, maybe thirteen. The sisters would take off their habits, they all had shiny blond hair that glowed with the rays of the sun shining in through the window and on them. I would have to make them feel good, while they beat me. I could take the pain, after a while, it would make my cock hard, but their tight, warm, holes, oh the feeling was wonderful," he says like he's reminiscing.

"Can you tell me how it all started?"

"After years of having the little boy fondle their breasts and touching their pussy, like he was petting a cat, they began to touch my cock when it was bigger. They would take turns stroking it and make me feel good, but when I came, they would beat me. Then they got even more creative, one sister would bend me over and stick a vibrator in my ass, while the other one jerked me off. Soon, they began letting me slide my cock inside their pussy, taught me how I should fuck them and make it feel good, but I wasn't allowed to come inside them. While I was cock deep in one's pussy, the other one was fucking my ass with a vibrator."

I watch as his face scrunches up, and I can see the struggle of the other Father Mullen trying to break through. "I'm not finished talking yet," the one known as demon said. "Eventually, I learned to hold my release, and I would fuck them so good, give them what they wanted. Touching, tasting, kissing, they always told me I was bad, I was a sinner, but they made us do this. They made me a devil. They would suck my cock, allowing me to go deep in their throats, while they gagged on me. Oh, that was a wonderful feeling. I have always loved when they suck me off."

"Oh, my goodness," Michelle whispers. "He was basically molested, raped, and abused as a child."

I can only nod my head.

The other Father comes through, breathing hard from fighting with the other one, "I became a priest once I was of age, and for a while, everything was good while I was in the Church and away from the orphanage, but then I was allowed to go out and wander the areas, that's when the demon came back."

"How did he choose his victims?" Kim asks.

"We would walk to a park that had a lake, we would walk the jogging path, and if a blond female jogged by us, he watched and waited, six counts of her passing. If she was alone on the sixth time he saw her, he would jump out, hit her in the head once to knock her off her feet, then he'd hit her on the side of the head to knock her out," he takes a deep breath, trying to control the demon inside him. I can see the battle he is having as his face continues to scrunch up like he is in massive amounts of pain.

"He would carry them through the bushes, towards the lake by trees. He threw their cell phone in the lake, stripped them of their clothes, took our robe off, opened their legs, and slid my penis inside them, then he would play with their breasts, before putting his mouth over their nipples. When they would come to, he would continue going deeper, saying dirty things to them as they'd try to fight him," he tells us.

I look over at Michelle as she puts her hand on her breast, like she is trying to cover it up.

"Did he do something to you?" I ask, needing to know.

"He latched his mouth to my breast as I was coming to from being knocked out," she says, scrunching her face in disgust as she remembers the feeling.

I look back at the man sitting at the table and want to kill him for touching what is mine. I can feel my anger rising, and I guess Michelle could too, because she placed her hand over my heart and said, "I'm fine, I'm here."

That's true, she is here, and she is alive, but I'm still pissed he touched her. I watch fascinated as the demon quickly takes over.

"Oh, it was so much more than that. I fucked them deep and good, not just in their warm pussy, but I took their ass, while holding onto their blond locks, and when I was done with that, they would suck my cock until I made them choke and suffocate. Nothing like watching their face turn blue, while taking my cock deep into their throats. Mmmm, God I'm so hard right now," he says disgustingly.

"When was the first time you killed?"

"At the orphanage before I left. One nun wanted to have a little afternoon delight while the other nun was busy doing something else. She was sucking my cock, and it felt so good, the vibrations of her gagging, as well as feeling the back of her throat with the head of my cock. I wanted to get deeper, so I grabbed the back of her head, and I continued shoving her head on my cock as I got deeper and deeper into her throat. I was so lost in the feeling of wanting to come but being trained not to, so I kept going. I didn't even notice when she was beating on my legs, or when she turned blue until I finally came down her throat with my release. I looked down to see if I would be punished, and she was simply dead," he says casually.

"What did you do then?"

"I got her dressed, laid her in the bed, and left that night."

"How many others have you killed?"

"I don't know, it's hard to keep track of numbers when you've been to fourteen different states," the demon says nonchalantly.

"Do you remember all the states you've been to?"

"Of course, we were in California, Arizona, Colorado, Georgia, Alabama, Florida, South Carolina, Illinois, Ohio, Montana, Michigan, New York, Connecticut, and now Maine."

"Why put them in the lake?" Kim asks.

"That was the other fool, it was his way of baptizing them and ensuring God took their souls, but he fails to realize I already have their souls, especially that sweet virgin I took. Damn, she made me do things I hadn't enjoyed since I was a teenager with those virgin nuns."

"What did you do with their clothes?"

"I put them in the lakes, held down by rocks."

"What about the nipples you cut off?"

He pulls out a zip lock bag from his robe, "You mean these? They are always with me. I like to play with them as I wait for the next one."

"Good Lord," I hear Frankie say, "That's a lot of victims."

"Did you not pat him down?" I ask angrily.

"Of course we did, Boss, for weapons, we didn't find anything. Apparently, there are more hiding places in the Father's robe than we realized," Frankie says.

I can only nod my head in agreement, since indeed it would seem that way if the Father was able to pull those out from somewhere in his robe. "He needs to be searched again," I say seething.

I pull my wife into my side, knowing she could have been one of his victims, and that scares the living hell out of me. *What if we would have been a few minutes later getting to her? I can't allow myself to think about the what if's. She's here beside me, and alive. That's what I need to focus on.*

I watch as Kim gets up from the table, grabbing the zip lock bag, and leaving the father in the room. She walks into the room we are in and says, "He will need to go to a State Mental Facility, but I am very concerned. One feels guilty, and the other sees nothing wrong with what he has done. In fact, he enjoys it too much," Kim says, and I agree.

I watch through the two-way glass as Heath and Declan go back into the room and search Father Mullen again.

"Call the hospital and see if they have a solitary confined room they can put him in while he waits for trial. I'll call the DA in and brief him," I tell her.

"I just can't believe it. I watched him pray over his own victim," Michelle says. "I never thought when he said it was his fault he couldn't save her, he meant literally it was his fault," she adds, shock evident in her voice.

"Now we have him, and he will not hurt anyone else," I tell her, before saying, "Let's go home."

Chapter Twenty-Six

ERIC

One month later

We finally got a DNA match on the victim from Chester County, her name was Chelsea Yates. No one reported her missing because the only family she has is an Aunt who is in assisted living and wasn't aware that her niece was missing.

Father Mullen is tucked in the state mental hospital for the rest of his life. He was, of course, found incompetent to stand trial, but the families are happy knowing he will never get out. That will not bring back their loved ones, but knowing he had been caught was enough. When we looked into the states that he named off, we found approximately sixty-seven women whose murder fit the description of our serial killer's MO.

Michelle is doing better mentally after what happened with Father Mullen. Physically, she only had a few cuts and bruises, but mentally, she had nightmares for a couple of weeks, and I would be there to hold her. Though nothing happened to her, she always dreamt that we didn't save her in time. I made her go talk to a therapist, and she has helped Michelle see that what she is really dreaming about is survivor's guilt because we did save her, but no one saved the other girls. Once Michelle realized she was right, the nightmares have started to slowly fade. She still has one occasionally.

Detective Burton's granddaughter is still missing. One of her friends came forward and said the last they saw her, she was getting on a train to New York, but there is no record of her making it to New York. Detective Burton was finally able to get the data on her cell phone, it showed her phone last pinged off a tower in Boston before it went black. He has called in every agency from Boston to New York to help him search for his granddaughter.

There is only two months until Michelle and I have our second wedding. She and Kim are in complete planning mode and have decided we will cater a dinner for the gang. I have agreed to whatever she wants since this wedding is more for her than me. We did it my way the first time, and I want her to have the wedding she has always wanted.

Our families are also coming in for the occasion, even though they know we are already married.

I have decided since my brother was my bestman last time, I would ask Declan to be my best man this time, especially since Kim is the maid-of-honor, and I have a feeling there is something going on between those two. I spoke to my brother, and he was okay with that.

Michelle comes walking through the door after her run with Kim, Heath, and Frankie.

"Hey babe," I call out.

"Hi," she says, walking into the kitchen.

"Dinner is almost ready, you should go jump in the shower," I tell her.

"Want to join me?" she asks, leaning up for a kiss.

"Mmmm, absolutely," I say, turning the burner off and following her to the bedroom.

I start the shower, and her phone rings. She looks at the caller id and mouths Declan.

I look at her questioningly, and she shrugs her shoulders as she answers, "Declan, what's going on?"

"No, she's not with me, and we don't have plans to meet tonight."

"What do you mean she's gone?"

Michelle hits the speaker phone so I can hear as well.

"Her car is here at the house, but she is not. I called her phone, and it went straight to voicemail. We were supposed to have dinner tonight and she knew I was going to pick her up," fear is evident in his voice as he speaks.

"So why did you think she would be with me?" I hear Michelle ask with a worried tone in her voice as well.

"I just hoped maybe she got tied up with you on some wedding things, but you say no, and I don't know where else she could be, I'm concerned," he says, sounding more than concerned.

"Declan, you said her car is there?" I ask, cutting in, trying to remain calm.

"Yes, Boss. It's parked in the driveaway and locked."

"Did you go inside and see if anything is out of place?"

"Yes, Boss. Her keys are on the table by the door, with her purse, but I don't see her phone, and nothing else looks to be disturbed," he says, worry lacing his voice.

"Did you try to track her phone?"

"Yes, sir, and it's not registering, telling me it's off."

"Let me call Frankie and Heath and see if she said anything to them before she left the park," Michelle says, hanging up on Declan to call Frankie.

I pull my phone out and run a location check on Kim, but nothing is showing, just as Declan said. That's not like Kim, and worry punches me in the gut for my Agent and friend.

"Hello," he answers and it sounds like he's driving.

"Frankie, it's Michelle, did Kim tell you if she was going anywhere or had something to do before she left the park?"

"She was going home as far as I know, she didn't say she was doing anything else. Why?"

"She's not at home, but her car is there, and her phone is off, which is unlike her."

"Maybe she ran down to the store and didn't bother to drive," he says.

"Maybe. Thanks," Michelle says, hanging up.

She calls Heath next.

"Shelly, what's going on?"

"Did Kim say anything to you about going anywhere tonight?"

"No, why? What's going on?" he asks.

"She's not at home, but her car and stuff is there," she tells him.

"Did you call Frankie?"

"Yeah, he said she may have walked to the store. I'll have someone check it out."

"Okay, let me know."

I come back from turning off the shower to find her calling Declan back.

"Do they know anything?" He asks as soon as he answers the phone.

"Did you check the grocery store down from her house to ensure she didn't walk down there?" Michelle asks quickly.

"No, but I'll head that way now," he says.

"Call me back," Michelle tells him.

She looks at me. "I have a bad feeling, Eric. Kim never turns her phone off," Michelle says with tears in her eyes.

"It's okay, I'm sure she is safe," I tell her, while trying to keep my own fear at bay until I know more.

Fifteen minutes later, Declan calls back.

"She's not at the grocery store, or at any of the shops. No one has seen her today," he says frantically.

"Call the team and tell them to meet at the office. One of our own is missing, and we need to find out why," I say, grabbing Michelle as she starts to fall.

"What's happened to Kim?" she whispers as the tears fall down her face.

"I don't know, Shell, but we will find her. We need to go, and we all need to put our heads together to bring her home," I tell her and watch as she steels herself and nods.

I'm trying to be the strength that she needs, even though internally, I feel like a boulder has been placed on my chest. This panic is nothing like when my wife went missing, but it's close. Kim is not only my wife's best friend, but she is my right arm at work. I know I can trust her, and now she needs us to find out what happened to her. I have to keep a clear head.

"We will find her," Michelle says, "We will find her," she says again to herself over and over, almost as if she needs the mantra, and it breaks my heart to see my wife like this.

"She's strong, babe. If something has happened, she will fight."

"What if she can't?" she whispers, breaking down again.

"She's your best friend and a damn good agent, she will find a way," I tell her, trying to sound reassuring.

She nods her head, and we leave heading to the office.

What could have happened and who is responsible? I think to myself.

Kim, where are you?

Acknowledgements

To my support group, Kerrie, Carli, Dawn, Angel, Renea, and Mikki. Thank you, ladies, so much for all your love and help with my books and keeping me straight. These books wouldn't be what they are without all of you. Thank you from the bottom of my heart.

Mikki, thank you for all you do for me when I ask. You are a lovely, hardworking PA, and I can't tell you how much appreciated you are.

To all my ARC readers, I know I say it every time, but I seriously cannot thank you enough for all the love you show to me and my books.

To you, the readers, thank you for reading my book. I hope you enjoy reading this series as much as I'm enjoying writing it. If you loved Run To Murder, I ask that you take a moment and leave a review and let your friends know how much you enjoyed it.

XOXO,
Bella

Special thanks to:

Getcovers.com for the Cover Design

Horus Copyedit and Proofreading for editing

Proofreading and other Author Services by Renea for proofreading

About the author

I'm an author of steamy suspenseful romance novels, who loves to keep her readers guessing.

I have always loved the idea of happy endings, but with real life drama.

I currently live in North Carolina and have always loved the beauty of the Appalachian Mountains. Hiking is one of my favorite hobbies as it helps to clear my mind and allow my imagination to roam freely.

I'm an avid reader of all genres.

I love traveling, especially to small communities, as the people are always so nice and welcoming, with hidden gems in their sweet little towns.

Come follow me to learn more.

Facebook Reader Group - Bella's Romance Readers | Facebook

Instagram – https://www.instagram.com/author_bella_lane/

Website - https://www.bellalanebooks.com

Also by

BELLA LANE

<u>Men of Special Ops Forces</u>
Stroke of Midnight (Roman and Jessi's story)

Driving Home for Christmas (Nico and Sarah's story)

His Christmas Baby (Jonathan and Shawna's story)

A Soldier's Secret Romance (Ryan and Ellie's story)

Saved by the Major (Noah and Amanda's story)

Claiming Homebase (Justin and Livia's story)

Finding Ireland (Liam and Ireland's story)

The General's Secret (Connor and Destiny's story)

<u>Top Grunt Services Series</u>
Protected by the Bodyguard (Scott and Brianne's story)

Falling for the Bodyguard (Brody and Cami's story)

Loving the Bodyguard (Jax and Lena's story)

Shielded by the Bodyguard (Matt and Alisa's story)

<u>Heroes of Maine Series</u>
Defending Charley (Derrick and Charlene's story)

Saving Sam (Connor and Samantha's story)

Protecting Leia (Noah and Leia's story)

Healing the Quarterback (Will and Krista's story)

Saving St. Nicolas (Mike and Riley's story)

His Curvy Surprise

<u>Behavioral Unit Maine Series</u>
Run To Murder